lex Amit

Copyright © 2022 by Alex Amit
All rights reserved. This book or any portion thereof
may not be reproduced or used in any manner whatsoever
without the express written permission of the publisher
except for the use of brief quotations in a book review.

Printed in the United States of America

First Printing, 2022
Line Editing: Grace Michaeli

Contact: alex@authoralexamit.com
http://authoralexamit.com/

ISBN: 9798367786613

Wandering Birds

Alex Amit

To T.A., Who never gives up

The Old Display Cabinet
September 2021, Kyiv, Ukraine

Anna

"Grandma, it's me, Anuchka," I knock on Grandma Mariusha's gray wooden door, as I ignore the neighbor's look. The neighbor is standing at the end of the long corridor, peeking at me from her front door.

"She can't hear you, she never does," she says. However, I don't answer her. After a moment, she goes back inside and slams her apartment door. There's always some neighbor who has something to say.

"Grandma, open up. It's me," I remove my pink woolen gloves and knock on the wooden door again. I'll wait for a while. It always takes her time to open the door.

The hallway in the large apartment building isn't heated, and the cold autumn wind seeps through the small broken window at the end of the corridor. I rub my hands together, trying to warm them up. Maybe she's fallen asleep. I could tell Mom that I tried, and she didn't open up the door.

"Who's there?" I hear her slippers dragging on the floor through the thin wooden door.

"Grandma Mariusha, it's me."

"Anuchka?"

"Yes, it's me," I tuck my pink woolen gloves into my coat pocket.

I can hear the sound of the latch as she cracks the door open and examines me before she opens it wide and hugs me as I enter the small living room.

Her hair, which used to be black, has turned silver over the years, and her fast walk has now become slow. But her blue eyes and light skin haven't changed. I like to look at her old pictures, perched up in the old glass display cabinet against her living room wall. She was once a beautiful woman. Even today, to me, she's still beautiful.

"How are you, Anuchka?" She wraps her hands around me, and I can smell the sweet scent of the *Oludashki* from her hands as she presses me to her large breasts. "Did Mom send you?"

"Yes, she wanted to see if you were okay." Ever since I can remember, she smelled like cooked food. There was always something delicious cooking in her small apartment. The *Oludashki* is my favorite; airy pancakes, sprinkled with powdered sugar on top and sometimes, she serves them with her very own handmade cherry jam.

"Your mother worries too much. Tell her she doesn't need to worry about me. I have something for you to eat. Why didn't you tell me you were coming? I would have prepared more food." She turns to the small kitchenette. She has been living here by herself for years, ever since the government had given her this small apartment. It was all but a small guest room, one bedroom, and a kitchenette.

"How do you feel?" I follow her and watch as she struggles to hold onto the box of matches in her fist. "Let me help you." She is very old, and Mom asked me to stop by her place on my way back from the university and help her. I was supposed to keep her company until the evening.

"No need, Anuchka, I'm fine. I'll make you some tea." She leaves the matchbox on the counter and tries to light one of the matches, breaking it in the process.

"I'm not thirsty, but I'll stay and sit with you," I lie to her since I don't want her to strain herself.

"I prepared your favorite food!" She smiles at me as she comes in from the small kitchen, holding the plate of *Oludashki* sprinkled with snow-white sugar, and placing the plate on the coffee table.

We sit and watch the news segment, but after a while, I notice that she has fallen asleep on her brown recliner and is breathing peacefully. She'll probably wake up in a few hours. What should I do? I promised Mom that I would stay with her until the evening.

I pick up one *Oludashki* and taste it. Then I pace the room and look around.

Her dark eyes stare at me from the picture in the glass cabinet, as if smiling and inviting me to smile back at her. Her liquor bottles, kept locked behind the glass doors, also call out to me. I've been watching them ever since I was a young girl. I was told that I wasn't allowed to open the locked glass door, but I'm all grown up now, and back in the dorms, we drink almost every night. Where's the key? I look around; I think it'll be some time before she wakes up.

My fingers fumble around the top of the cabinet's wooden frame, which was too high for me when I was a child. I continue until I feel the metal touch of the key and smile to myself. I'm all grown up now. I'm allowed to open the forbidden cabinet.

I look at her before turning back to the glass doors, gently turning the key in the lock so it won't make a sound and wake Grandma up. Slowly I open the glass doors wide. I just have to make sure to be quiet.

There's one photograph of Maria Yfimovna, whom everyone calls Mariusha, and I call Grandma, and next to it a photo of her long-lost husband. They're both looking at me with severity. There are a few bottles of vodka. I grab one, and take a sip, ignoring the burning sensation in my throat. There's an old harmonica, some porcelain miniatures, and a mahogany-colored wooden box with a small latch and a drawer at its bottom.

My fingers flip the small latch over as I take another sip from the vodka. I smile at the sight of the open wooden lid and the tiny dancer who begins to spin in the music box, her hand raised over her head as she dances to the music. What's in the wooden drawer?

"Anuchka, is that you? What's this music?" I hear Grandma.

"It's nothing, Grandma," I shut the lid and fold the dancer back into the dark box, restoring the silence to the living room.

"Anuchka, is that the music box?"

"No, Grandma. I'm sorry," I put the bottle back in its place. I shouldn't have opened the cabinet.

"Anuchka, put it back. You know you're not allowed to touch the cabinet." She rises from the couch. Will she smell the vodka I drank?

"Yes, Grandma," I open the music box's small wooden drawer for a brief moment. Inside, I find a black and white photo of a woman dressed in a cream-colored dress, leaning on a motorcycle.

"Anuchka, sweetheart, put it back where you found it," she's standing beside me.

"Is that you, Grandma? Did you have a motorcycle when you were young?" The woman in the picture doesn't look like her.

"No, Anuchka, it's not me."

"So, who is she?" I take the old yellowing photo out of the drawer, feel the touch of the rough paper, and turn it over. There's something written on the back of the picture, but I can only read the word "Francesca" before Grandma snatches it out of my hand.

"It's a long story," she says slowly as she holds the photo in her wrinkled palm and returns it to the wood drawer.

"And what is it? Is it from the Great Patriotic War?" I pull a medal out of the drawer. It's red and star shaped. There are several other medals under it. "I thought you hated the Russians."

"Yes, my Anuchka, it's from the Great Patriotic War. Now put everything back in place, and I'll make you some tea."

"Were you there too? Were you fighting the Germans? Were you a communist like the Russians?"

"I don't want to talk about it, sweetheart. I don't want to talk about it." She takes the wooden box from my hands and holds it for a moment with trembling fingers.

"Why not? Why don't you like the Russians? Why don't you attend the parades like all the old war heroes with the medals on their chests? Why don't you talk about it?" I take out the rest of the medals and look at them. One is etched with a golden hammer and sickle, and another features several soldiers wearing helmets and holding rifles.

"Have you ever seen old people like me talking about it? They go to parades and sit in the grandstand in the cold April wind, drinking vodka and saying those were the good days, but have you ever seen any of them talk?" She gently takes the medals from me, and momentarily, I can feel her warm fingers. "I don't hate the Russians, I was part of them, but I don't trust them."

"Why don't you trust them?"

"Because that's how it is. Back then, they had Stalin who claimed that Ukraine belonged to him, and now they have someone else who claims that Ukraine belongs to him; I don't trust them. Anuchka, you're too young, you won't understand it."

"So, who is the woman standing next to the motorcycle? And why were you a communist? Why do you have a red star medal?"

"Because I had to enlist when the Germans arrived. I had to fight for our nation."

"And were you proud to enlist?" I take the wooden box from her hands, put the rest of the medals back inside, close it again behind the glass door and lock it.

"I was just a young girl like you back then. I was dreaming about boys and love," she turns, hunched over, she heads towards the kitchen. "I never thought about the woman in the photo. I didn't think that far away from here; there are leaders who want to rule the world."

Winds of War
Fascist Italy, June 10, 1940

Francesca

'At Mussolini and the elected government's order, effective immediately, Italy has declared war.'

I watch the worker dressed in blue hanging the poster on the bulletin board, holding a brush, and applying a thick coat of glue from the bucket in his other hand.

Two or three more brush strokes of glue over the paper and he continues on his way down the street towards the village center. I stay behind to look at the new poster, droplets of the wet glue still glistening in the morning.

The street is quiet in the early morning, and I glance across the alley to see that no one is coming before I approach the bulletin board and pretend to read it.

There's an axe-bearing eagle sigil at the top of the poster, the symbol of the fascist party. The large black letters below announce that due to the alliance between Italy and the Nazis, from this moment on, the Italian army will assist the Germans in the war.

I glance one more time to ensure that the street is empty, and I get a little closer, as if struggling to read the letters that are still wet with glue. My fingernails quickly start peeling the poster off, tearing it into shreds. I need to hurry.

My fingers continue to tear long pieces from the paper and roll them into small balls, which I throw on the pavement, shaking them off my hands that are now sticky with glue. I work quickly, careful not to get my dress dirty. I have to watch out for police patrols. Recently they've restationed

Rome's police officers in our village. The village used to have a single policeman, but they'd replaced him, claiming he was no longer fit for his job.

"Don't do that. It's dangerous." I hear a voice behind me and quickly turn around. I need to run away.

"It's just paper. It's fine," I answer Insane Gabriele, who approaches and stands next to me. He bends down and starts picking up the sticky pieces of paper I've thrown on the pavement.

"Everything must be in order." He looks up at me with a serious expression. He gathers the sticky papers, trying to straighten the shreds.

He's about forty or fifty years old. He's always dressed in an old, tattered military coat and ragged shoes. His hair is unruly, and he reeks of sweat. Since I was a child, I remember him walking around the village square, strolling among the stalls, and shouting. Even then he was crazy, and all the kids would laugh at him.

"Get out of here," I say and start briskly walking away, leaving him crouched on the floor, playing with the papers. When I look back, I see him trying to stick them back onto the torn poster and rearrange them as they were.

A police whistle makes me hasten my steps. I take a turn into an alley and try walking at a normal pace. I straighten my dress, making sure I haven't stained it. My hands are still sticky. I need to wash them.

"There was a beautiful woman here. She told me to fix the poster." I can still hear Insane Gabriele as I continue walking. But after a couple of steps, I stop and turn back, peeking from the alley at the main street.

Two policemen in black uniforms are forcefully holding him up against the wall as he whimpers like an abandoned puppy. It isn't my concern. I should get out of here.

"He's insane. Leave him alone," I shout and swiftly run towards them. I bend down as he did before and pick up some of the pieces of the torn paper left on the pavement. I glue them back to the poster, dirtying my hands in the process, just so they won't suspect me.

"You're a good woman." Gabriele smiles at me as he tries to turn his head, despite the policeman's grip, pushing him against the wall.

"And who are you?" One of them asks me.

"I'm from this village, and he's insane. Leave him alone," I stand in front of him.

"Do you have a name?" The policeman asks with a mocking smile, continuing to hold Gabriele's head against the stone wall.

"Yes, I have a name," I raise my chin.

"And how should I call the lovely woman so keenly protecting such a dirty drunk?"

"Francesca, is that good enough for you?" I look at the policeman.

"So, why does a young woman such as yourself care about a madman like him?" He smiles at me. He has a black mustache and dark eyes.

"Leave him alone," I stare into the policeman's eyes, even though I should get away.

"Ask politely."

"Please, let him go." I stop myself from spitting at his feet.

His hand firmly grips the back of Gabriele's neck as he slowly scans my body. His eyes linger on my lips, wander to my breasts, down my summer dress and all the way down to my bare legs and my simple leather shoes. Only after he raises his gaze again and looks me in the eye, does he release Gabriele – but not before slapping the back of his head.

Gabriele falls to the ground as the other policeman laughs.

"We need to fix the poster," Gabriele continues to mumble as he remains lying on the cobblestones.

"Here, I released him. Can I buy you a cup of coffee?" The policeman ignores Gabriele and smiles at me as I continue to look at him; my gaze frantically jumping from one policeman to the other. I need to get out of here.

"No, I'm busy," I reply unsmilingly, turn around, and start heading towards the alley.

"Signorina," I can still hear him calling behind me. Insane Gabriele will have to take care of himself if they keep picking on him. I need to hurry up and wash my hands.

"Where have you been? I've been waiting for you," Cecilia kisses my cheek as I approach the fountain in the center of the square and hug her. She is twenty-two, like me, and we both have dark eyes and tanned skin after having spent hours under the Italian sun. She also has black hair like mine, although hers is curly and mine is wavy and long. We have known each other since we were little girls. We'd played together all the time. However, now, we're all grown up; we're done playing.

"I apologize. I got held up." I dip my hands into the stream of water flowing from the mouth of the marble lion erected at the top of the small fountain spitting a jet of water.

"Did you resist them again?"

"I helped our country," I reply quietly, not wanting all the other women by the fountain to hear us. They gossip, always telling each other everything.

"It's dangerous. They'll catch you in the end," she approaches me and whispers.

"I know how to be careful." I rub my fingers hard under the water, not telling her about Insane Gabriele and the cops.

"Did they put up new posters?"

"Yes, I've already taken care of them; I've torn their propaganda into strips, but that's not enough. We need to do more." I look around the square at the vegetable stalls and tomato trays drying in the sun.

Despite the early morning hour, the street corner café is already open. Some men are sitting there, perusing their morning newspaper, reading about the victories of the Italian army in Africa. Still, the women gather every morning near the fountain, whispering that the army's conditions in Africa are terrible. According to the rumors, there are many casualties in the battles, but the government hides this from the public while the generals award themselves honorary medals. Mussolini's giant poster, the Duce, also stares at us with a stern look from the cinema wall at the side of the square. Once, they used to feature romantic films, and they would hang a poster of a beautiful heroine kissing her lover; anything but Mussolini's ugly face. It's been months since a new movie arrived at the village. The only thing arriving these days is news and propaganda movies, glorifying the fascists, and telling of non-existent victories.

"Will you come in the evening to help me?" I ask her as we select vegetables from a produce stand.

"What do you want to do?" She looks to the sides.

"We have to do something." I pick a couple of tomatoes and put them in the basket. Later, I will drench them in salt and olive oil, then dry them in the sun.

"I'm not sure I can come." She also fills her basket with tomatoes.

"You must. We must do something."

"No, we don't. We're not children anymore, and this isn't a game."

"That's right, we're not children anymore. That's why we need to start making our voices heard because no one cares about us women," I finish filling my basket. "Bring your boyfriend along. He'll be on the lookout." I smile at her. I need her to come. I'm too scared to do it on my own.

"I might join you. And he isn't my boyfriend," she smiles and blushes as she shakes her head, shaking her curls every which way.

"Then just invite him over." I kiss her goodbye on the cheek. "See you in the evening," I start walking away before she changes her mind.

Carrying the vegetable basket on my shoulder, I hurry home. We might do something little more daring tonight than simply tearing the fascists' posters off a bulletin board.

Later that night, I lean on a stone wall in the alley leading to the square. I look at the black sky and wonder if she has changed her mind. The village is dark and quiet. Although the war hasn't reached us yet, since the war started, the Duce's government has announced a fuel rationing in preparation for the war. Most of the streetlights are off at night. The people also tend to close their shops early and hurry home, allowing packs of jackals to roam the streets. Under the cover of darkness, they come into the village from the fields surrounding it, searching for prey; just like the police patrols and the Blackshirts.

"They're worse than the jackals," I say to myself as I lean against the house's stone wall, listening for every noise.

I fight the urge to light a cigarette knowing that wouldn't be smart. If I did, I'd be standing out in the dark, flickering a small spot of light and blowing the cigarette's smell. It's better just to wait for her. She'll probably come soon.

In one hand, I'm holding the rolled-up leaflets I had written earlier by the lantern in the small wooden shed next to our house. My other hand is holding the glue can and brush. Could she have changed her mind?

"Francesca," I hear a whisper.

"I'm here," I step out of the shadows. I can recognize Cecilia approaching in the darkness, and a man follows her.

"I brought reinforcements." she hugs me.

"Does he know what we're planning to do?" I hand her the rolled-up posters with the anti-fascist slogans.

"He knows; he likes me." She quietly grins as she approaches me.

"The Duce wants to join the war with the Nazis," I whisper to the guy in the darkness, pronouncing Mussolini's nickname like a curse. I don't introduce myself. It's better that he doesn't know my name and that I don't know his.

"Take a look at what she wrote," Cecilia grabs one of the rolled-up leaflets and unfolds it under the faint moonlight, trying to show him the writing.

"The Duce wants us to sacrifice Italian blood so he can walk arm in arm with Hitler, review military parades, and rule the world," I continue to explain. I should have added those words to the leaflets. "And nobody cares." I take the sheets of paper from Cecilia's hands and roll them up again. "Nobody cares what we do here. We're just a small village south of Rome. Will you help us?"

"Yes," he whispers and takes another step towards Cecilia.

"Let's start," I hand him the can of glue and signal him to

walk in front of us. He starts to walk down the dark alley. We need to be more careful. The northern police officers have joined forces with the fascists.

We walk in silence. Only the sounds of our footsteps ring through the deserted street. We occasionally pass under an open window dimly lit by a kerosene lantern, but most of the blinds are closed and allow us to move in the dark. I can hear the jackals howling in the distance. They must be approaching through the dirt roads and stone terraces surrounding the village, looking for scraps of food.

"Here," I whisper to the guy walking ahead of me. He hands Cecilia the can of glue and hurries to the other side of the alley. If he notices anyone, he'll whistle, and if the police arrive, Cecilia and I will try to hide the posters under our dresses. They don't usually search on women's bodies.

I spread the poster on a stone wall while Cecilia applies it with the glue brush, gluing it to the wall. The wet bristles of the brush stroke my fingers as they hold up the poster, staining them with the thick, sticky glue.

"I'm done," she nods, and we rush to another stone wall, repeating the process.

"Come here!" I rush as we approach the dark village square after having hung several leaflets.

"It's dangerous," she approaches me. "Police officers sit here at night and smoke."

"I don't see any cigarette lights. They aren't here." I wave at the guy who's watching at the end of the alley. He approaches us and then goes out to patrol the square to make sure it's empty.

"It's risky," Cecilia says, slightly raising her voice and touching my hand. I can feel her hand's sweat and her body's warmth.

"We have to do it," I answer. I start to sweat too, despite the cool breeze. She mustn't think that I'm afraid. I mustn't think that I'm afraid.

"I'll do it myself if you're scared." I reach for the can when I notice the guy's silhouette, waving at us, signaling us the coast is clear. However, Cecilia continues to grip the can's thin metal handle and follows me as we enter the square.

The pavement stones glimmer under the moonlight. The sounds of our footsteps mix with the splashing water coming from the stone fountain at the center of the square. Even the jackals outside the village are silent now. Perhaps they returned to the fields.

At first, I plaster the last poster on the wall next to one of the shops, but then I change my mind. I head towards the cinema on the other side of the square.

Dressed in his military uniform and raising his hand in salute, Mussolini's huge poster is plastered all over the façade of the cinema painted on a rigid canvas. Even in the dark, I notice the brush strokes of his mouth, agape and roaring with enthusiasm, the bold letter above his image stating 'Duce.'

"Hurry up," I whisper to Cecilia as I stretch my arms as high as possible and smear the leaflet I wrote across his nose.

She approaches me, and her hands reach up as she applies the glue to the paper. I can hear her breathing and ignore the glue dripping down my arms. It's not important right now. What matters is that she finishes, and we manage to get out of the square.

"That's it. We did it," she dashes off, and I follow her, motioning for the young man to join us, stopping only for a moment to look back. Under the faint moonlight, our little leaflet is but a tiny speck on the huge nose of the monster saluting Sieg Heil, dominating the dark and deserted square.

"We need to stop this. We'll get caught." Cecilia says as we stand again in the dark alley, far away from the single lit streetlamp. "What we're doing is completely pointless. It changes nothing, and these policemen are here for a reason," she tries to catch her breath, making sure to stay in the shadows.

"You're right. It changes nothing," I take out a box of cigarettes and matches from my dress pocket, but after a moment, I change my mind and put the matches back. I don't want them to see my hands shaking. "It's no use," I continue talking, the unlit cigarette protruding from between my lips. I've been smoking for two years, ever since they knocked on our door and took my dad. I'm not afraid of them.

The guy hands me a lit match, and I draw nearer to his outstretched hand. I gratefully inhale the smoke, as I momentarily see his face in the light of the match before it goes off. He's looking at Cecilia.

"Good night," Cecilia whispers and walks away with him. "We agreed to stop."

"We need to do it in Rome," I whisper into the darkness, unsure if they heard me or had already walked away.

"Do you know what will happen to us if we get caught in Rome?" I see her silhouette turning around and approaching me. "They won't let us go. You know I'll do anything for you, but this is just too dangerous."

"Yeah, I know," I exhale the smoke and try to peel off the glue that stained my hands earlier and left an unpleasant layer on my fingers. In the distance, I can hear the jackals howling again. "I know what they're capable of." The day they took my dad was the last time I saw him.

"Rome has hundreds of police officers," the guy who lit the match for me says. "And informants, everywhere." He takes a step closer and stands at her side.

"They're too powerful," Cecilia adds.

"I thought you were against the war," I answer, even though I know they're right. The Blackshirts are too strong. My father also thought they were too strong. Still, he went out to protest.

"Aren't you afraid?" The young man looks at me.

"No, I'm not afraid." I'm glad that we're under the cover of darkness. "Will you two come with me to Rome?"

"We're not going to Rome. You hate Rome and all the rich people who live there," Cecilia says.

"Yes, I hate Rome. But you know I'm not going to give up, and I need you to come with me." I place my hand on hers. If she doesn't come with me, I won't have the courage to go to Rome by myself.

"We'll come with you," Cecilia finally says. "You know I'll join you. We're friends. But we'll have to be careful. Will you come with us?" She turns to the man, and he approaches her and holds her hand.

"Then it's settled. We go to Rome," I throw the cigarette on the pavement and crush it with my shoe. "If you're afraid, you'll be on the lookout, and I'll do what needs to be done."

"I'm scared. I hope you are too," Cecilia replies.

"See you tomorrow, and I'm not afraid." I don't hug her goodbye. I don't want her to notice my hands shaking in the dark.

"Run away!" I hear someone screaming the next day, and I drop the brush and paint can I had previously held in my hand. I can still see the black paint splattered on the wall of the Fascist Party building, forming an ugly stain, before I start running as fast as I can.

It was dangerous to arrive in Rome with ready-made leaflets. Policemen inspect people at the bus stations, inquiring about the purpose of their travel to the capital. Sometimes they also check their belongings. Before we boarded the bus to Rome, we decided to write a protest slogan on one of the city walls.

Run, Run, Run, don't stop, don't look back, ignore the whistle, ignore the businessmen in suits following me with their eyes. I cross the main street and pass an avenue of shops packed with goods despite the war that had started.

When we arrived in the city, I walked into one of those shops to purchase a can of black paint. We were afraid to take it with us on the bus so we wouldn't arouse any curiosity. Even though the salesman asked if I also needed a paintbrush, I told him no, so he wouldn't get suspicious. Then, we looked for another hardware store. But now it doesn't matter. They're after me.

Run, run, run, don't stop running.

My ribs ache with effort, and I'm panting. I can't stop. Every few seconds, I hear the police officers whistling behind me. I mustn't look back; it'll slow me down. I run past two cyclists and turn right into an alley. I stand there for a second, lean in and clasp my diaphragm. I need to throw up. But after a couple of breaths, I get up and continue running, ignoring the pain, passing two elegantly dressed women walking down the street as they stare at me suspiciously. Where are Cecilia and her friend? What happened to them?

We met at the village bus stop in the afternoon and waited for the bus to Rome. We sat in silence, and I felt they had changed their minds about the trip. I think Cecilia was doing this for me. But I didn't care. I wanted to protest, even if it was hopeless. I wanted the fascists to know that someone was opposing them. After we bought the paint and brush, we arrived at an alley adjacent to the Fascist Party's building. Cecilia and her friend stood at the corner of the alley to watch, and I began writing on the wall. But now it's too late. They disappeared, and the whistle continues to ring in my ears every few seconds. I stop, bend down to take a breath, get up and continue running again. Maybe it would have been better for them if they hadn't joined me at the village bus station and would have just left me there. If they wouldn't have come, I wouldn't have gone.

I run from the alley to a small square paved with stones, running between several cyclists. Two horse-drawn carts are standing at the side of the square, and I stop for a moment behind them. I crouch and hide, panting and wheezing.

My hands are pressed against my diaphragm, and I suddenly notice the black stains on my fingers. I have to clean them. My dress is also stained with black paint that had probably spattered off the wall when I threw the can of paint away before I fled. What am I going to do?

One of the horses neighs. I look up and see two policemen walking on the other side of the square, inspecting the shops. I approach the horse, caress its muzzle, and look into its brown eyes. Maybe they'll think I'm the owner of the cart.

I continue to stroke the horse's brown coat, letting it sniff my paint-covered fingers and the strong scent emanating from them as I follow the police officers with my eyes.

Please don't suspect me. Keep walking, don't come here.

The sound of footsteps behind me makes me look away from the policemen, and I see a man in work clothes approaching me, examining me.

"What are you doing? Why are you petting the horse?" he asks me.

What should I answer him?

"I need help," I whisper.

"Get out of here," he raises his voice.

"Sorry, I'll go." I hurry away from him, trying to walk as normally as I can. If I start running, the police will come to check why that man had yelled. I need to find a hiding place to stay at until the evening. Then I'll look for a way to return to the village.

Hours later, at night, I come out of my hiding place and start searching for the bus station. I have no idea where I am, and I start walking slowly in the nearly empty streets. My body aches from hours of sitting crammed between empty wooden crates in one of the alleys. I stop for a moment next to one of the fountains. I try to clean my hands as best I can and drink from the water, despite its bitter taste. I haven't eaten all day. Every now and then, I look around, scanning for police officers or the Blackshirt thugs. They're the most dangerous ones.

The marble sculpture overlooking the fountain and the pool below seems to look down on me with a stern look. I shouldn't have offered Cecilia and the other guy to come to Rome with me. What happened to them? Did they get caught?

I dip my palms into the pool and leave them there for a while .The feeling of the icy water soothes me, and I wet my sweaty forehead. I should have listened to Cecilia and stayed in the village. There's no point in trying to fight them. They're just too strong. I dip my palms in the water for one last time and continue to walk down the street, looking for the bus station.

The streetlamps illuminate the fascist party flags hanging from multiple balconies, proudly waving in the night breeze, and the large Duce posters calling for war are plastered on every street corner. What will I do if they didn't manage to escape and the Blackshirts caught them near the party building? I can't even think about it. I need to ask someone for directions to the bus station, but I'm afraid. My dress is stained with black paint; they'll surely suspect me.

It's almost midnight when I find the bus station, but all the platforms are already abandoned, and the square is deserted. I sit down on a bench and look around. Only the newsstand and the café on the other side of the square are open. Several people are sitting at the tables, but Cecilia and the other guy aren't among them. They've probably already boarded the earlier bus heading south of Naples, on their way back to the village. All they did was stand at the street corner; they didn't hold the brush, or the paint can, nor paint the protest slogan on the building. No one had reason to suspect them. I'm so hungry, what am I going to do?

"There are no more buses at this time. Try tomorrow," the man at the newspaper stand says. I thank him as I keep standing next to the booth, looking at the newspaper hanging in front of the stand. 'Italy and Germany Formed an Alliance,' the headlines scream. What will I do tonight?

I wonder if I should answer him, but then I hear a whistle and footsteps, and I look back, frantically searching where I should run to. A group of Blackshirts enter the square, singing the fascist anthem and drumming loudly. I hid behind the stand and my body tensed up. They're sitting at the café on the other side of the square, loudly ordering wine. Some of the people at the café join them in song and start clapping. I should prepare to run again. Will I be doing this all night?

I pretend to read a newspaper by the stand and ignore the stand owner, who has started folding the newspapers into the stand, preparing to close for the night.

A motorcycle roars by and surprises me. My body tenses up again. However, I have nowhere to go but stand close to the almost closed newsstand. A young man on a red motorcycle pulls over and rushes to the newsstand seller, who's leaning down boarding up his booth.

"Cigarettes, please," he hands the seller a bill, and the seller silently gets up and walks into the booth.

"You're late. I've been waiting for a long time," I say to the man and step out of the shadows. I can't stay here, so close to the Blackshirt pack sitting at the café.

He just looks at me and doesn't say a thing. I look back

at him, seeing his dark wild hair and black eyes shine under the streetlamp's faint light. He has to help me.

"Have a good night," the seller says to him and hands him his cigarettes and change.

"Please," I whisper softly to the man, as I gesture with my head at the Blackshirts sitting in the square and show him my stained dress and palms. I failed to clean them in the fountain water.

"Thank you, good night," he says to the newspaper seller and turns his back to me, sits back on the motorcycle, starts it with a jerk, and the air is once again filled with the bike's monotonous rumble and the smell of gasoline.

"Are you coming?" He turns his gaze to me, raising his voice over the motorcycle's noise.

"What's your name?" He shouts out as we drive through the streets. I wrap my arms tightly around him, so I won't fall. My head is close to his, but I don't answer him, pretending I didn't hear the question.

We're so close, I can feel the touch of his leather jacket through the thin fabric of my dress. What does he think about me?

"Are you hungry?" He asks a couple of minutes after we drive past an open bakery. Even though I don't want to answer him, I shout "yes." I'm so hungry

"Wait here." He pulls over, walks into the bakery, and comes out after a moment. He hands me some cookies and a pastry with sesame seeds.

"Where do you need to go?" He asks as we eat standing next to his motorcycle.

"Far," I answer him, watching as he lights himself a cigarette. I don't want to ask him for one. Women aren't supposed to smoke.

"You came all the way to Rome, and now you're running away from the Blackshirts?" He scans my stained dress.

"That's none of your business."

"You're on my motorcycle, so it's my business too. Why are you running away from them?"

"Thank you for your motorcycle." I touch the warm motorcycle leather seat. "I'll continue on my own from here." I turn around and start walking down the street. It's better to manage alone than stay with him and his motorcycle if he's going to ask me all these questions. Maybe he's also one of them, and he momentarily felt sorry for me. I don't need a man who thinks he has to protect me.

"Hey, wait," he yells after me.

"What?" I turn to him.

"Do you think you stand a chance?"

"A chance in what?"

"A chance to go home, a chance against them."

"I've known how to get back home even before I met you." I approach him. "And I'll know how to get back home even after you leave. Can I have a cigarette, please?" I hold out my hand. I don't care what he thinks of me.

"And against them? Do you think you stand a chance against them?" He takes the pack of cigarettes out of his leather jacket pocket and lights a match, waiting for me to lean into his hands while he protects the small flame.

"Maybe you're one of them," I blow the smoke and look at him.

"Yeah, maybe I'm one of them," he watches me and returns the cigarettes into his pocket. "My family is definitely part of them. Have a nice walk home," he turns his back to me and sits back on his motorcycle.

"I know it's hopeless, but I won't give up," I say to him almost in a whisper, even though I shouldn't. If he rats me out, I'll end up locked in their basements.

He sits there with his back to me but doesn't start. I hear a car driving down the road. "When I was a child, my dad would attend protests," I continue talking, moving closer to him so I wouldn't have to shout. "The Blackshirts pounded him with their blows." I spit on the ground when I say their name. It doesn't matter, in any case, he'll soon speed off on his ugly motorcycle. "Then they came and took him for questioning. You can go and report now to the party's headquarters or your family that you've found a traitor." I throw at him the paper bag with the pastry and cookie leftovers. I see it hitting his back, turn on my heels, and walk down the street. "Thanks for the food," I shout without turning around, and inhale the bitter cigarette smoke. I'll find my way back to the village. It's not far from Rome.

"And what happened to your father?" He approaches me a minute later and raises his voice. He's still riding his noisy motorcycle as I walk on the sidewalk and watch him.

"That's none of your business. I'm sure you can check it out at the fascist party's headquarters. You probably know where it is." I keep going. I don't need his pity.

"What did you say your name was?"

"I didn't say." I shout over the motorcycle's humming engine.

"You won't stop the war."

"I know." I finally face him, looking into his dark eyes. Is he looking down on me?

"You won't be able to avenge him either." He doesn't smile, just looks at me with a serious look.

"I know."

"Are you cold?"

"A little."

"Take this," he takes off his leather jacket and hands it to me. I take a step to the road and take the jacket from his outstretched hand. When I wear it, I can still feel the warmth of his body replacing the autumn chill.

We watch each other in silence, the only sound cutting through it the motorcycle's grumble, as if waiting for something to happen. Finally, I throw the cigarette on the pavement, hop on the motorcycle behind him, and hug him tightly, shouting the name of my village over the whistling wind.

Later, when we're driven out of Rome, racing on the dark road, with nothing but the motorcycle's headlights casting a faint yellow beam on the asphalt, I whisper my name too, making sure he won't hear it. He must have saved me out of pity, and maybe tomorrow he'll inform the Blackshirts. It's better that he doesn't know my name and that we never meet again. I close my eyes and try to think about Cecilia and the other guy, but all I can think about is my arms wrapped around him and the warmth of his body.

"Cecilia," I whisper and throw a small stone at her bedroom window. Is she home?

The stone hits the closed shutters and makes a faint sound as it falls back onto the paved street. "Cecilia," I throw another one and whisper louder in the dark. Did they make it back to the village? Is she okay?

Right after he dropped me off in the village, I rushed to her house. I said goodbye to him and refused to tell him my name.

"Cecilia," I whisper again, but only an owl hoots back at me, the sound of its wings rustling in a nearby cypress tree. Maybe they were caught? Why did I take them with me to that horrible city? The motorcyclist insisted on handing me a note with his address and phone number before he left. However, I refused, stating I would tear it up the moment I hear him drive away on his noisy motorcycle. He just smiled and told me that we would meet again, and drove down the road and left the village, illuminating the darkness with his motorcycle headlights as if he were a star growing smaller and smaller until he disappeared around the bend. I won't see him again anyway.

"Cecilia," I throw a larger stone that hits the shutters and rings through the silence of the street. I don't have the courage to knock on her door if she isn't there. What will I tell her parents?

The wooden door creaks open, and I see her silhouette approaching me. I think she's wearing a robe. She ties the belt around her waist.

"Cecilia, are you okay?" I try to hug her in the dark, but she recoils.

"They almost caught me."

"I'm sorry."

"I was lucky to have him with me. We pretended we were a couple. He hugged me, and even though they suspected us, they finally let us go. I would have been in their basements if he hadn't joined with me." She keeps her distance from me.

"I didn't mean for it to end like this, but we have to do anything we can to stop the war," I say and hear howling jackals outside the village.

"You're so naïve. Do you think that paint of yours will change something?"

"Maybe if there were more women like us, it would make a change."

"Women have never changed a thing," she says. "And I think we shouldn't talk anymore about what happened. Even in our village, there are people who support the fascists."

"Are we still friends?" I reach my hands out to her.

"We're still friends," she responds to my plea, and I feel her warm fingers holding mine.

"Did he hug you?" I try to change the subject.

"Yes, he has strong arms." I see her white teeth gleaming in the dark as she smiles and describes how he leaned in and kissed her in front of the police officer who watched them suspiciously.

I also want to tell her about how I ran away and how I returned to the village. But she didn't ask, and I know that anyway, I'll never see the motorcycle rider again.

"Good morning," he tells me a couple of days later. I have no idea how long he has been waiting for me in the alley near my house, but when I open the door leading to the street, I see him leaning against his red motorcycle and smiling politely at the neighbors peeking at him through their windows.

I stand by the door at the top of the stone stairs leading to the alley and contemplate what to do. I momentarily fight the urge to go back inside and slam the door behind me, but then I raise my chin and walk towards him. I try to accentuate my curves under my simple dress.

"I forgot to get your name," he walks towards me and smiles. He seems too embarrassed to extend his hand for a shake, as if he's afraid it would be too formal. But I walk past him, pretending I haven't noticed him. His new red motorcycle sparkles in the morning sun and stands out compared to an old wooden cart parked on the street.

"You traveled all the way from Rome just to know my name?" I keep walking towards the village square as he walks beside me. He's wearing the leather jacket that he offered me the other day, and in daylight, I try to sneak glances at him and examine his face. He's taller than me and his complexion is slightly lighter than mine. His black hair is beautiful and neat, brushed back with gel as if he had come out of a magazine; the motorcycle ride from Rome didn't seem to have any effect on him. Perhaps he visited the village barbershop before he positioned himself at my front door. His cheeks are also neatly shaved.

"I wanted to make sure that you've made it home safe and sound. It was late when you left that night, and yes, I also wanted to ask for your name. You didn't tell me what it is." He keeps walking beside me. As we walk side by side, I try to smell his scent, the one I breathed in only a couple of nights ago, when I hugged his waist on the motorcycle. But we're too far apart, and I can't.

"My name is Francesca," I whisper, making sure he doesn't hear it. "And I'm fine, thanks," I continue walking.

"Can I take you for coffee?" He continues walking beside me. He probably didn't tell his family that he was going to meet a villager.

"Why did you come here?" I stop and turn to him, looking into his dark eyes.

"I would like to take you for coffee," he smiles at me.

"I'm not like your family."

"I'm not my family."

"This isn't Rome. This is a small village."

"And this small village doesn't have any cafés?"

"A small village doesn't have fancy shops like Rome, and the café here is simple unlike the fancy ones in Rome. We don't have any rich families here like you do in Rome; all those rich families who have a phone at home and money to buy noisy motorcycles that stink up the air with gasoline."

"That's right, you're right," he stops smiling, "in Rome, women have manners. If someone offers to take a woman in Rome for coffee, she says, 'thank you' and has a cup of coffee. Sometimes it's nice to get to know someone just because they're interesting, even if they aren't like all the rich people from Rome." He turns around and starts walking back up the alley towards his motorcycle.

"Francesca. My name is Francesca," I cry out and ignore an elderly woman passing by the alley, pulling a mare straddled with firewood for winter.

"Nice to meet you, Francesca," he answers without facing me and continues walking towards his motorcycle.

"And I'm not coming to Rome with you," I shout at his back. In a moment, he'll disappear around the corner. "And what's your name? What kind of family do you have in Rome?" I start following him.

The Old Photo
September 2021, Kyiv, Ukraine

Anna

Francesca Morelli. That's all the words I can read in that foreign language written on the back of the old photograph of the woman. Probably, the rest of the words indicate the place's name and date - November 1940.

I walk from Grandma Mariusha's house towards the metro and the train that will take me to the student dorm. I zip up my pink leather jacket to protect myself from the autumn wind and look again at the black and white photo. The woman in the picture is standing next to the motorcycle. She has long black hair, and she's smiling at me, or rather the person who took the picture many years ago. I'll return it tomorrow when I visit grandma again. Grandma doesn't need to know that I took it, even though she had asked me to put the wooden box back in its place.

As I wait for the train at the metro station, I once again take the photo out of my pocket and look at it. I can't identify the square or the surrounding buildings. It doesn't look like a building in Kyiv to me. I turn the photo over again, but I can't understand the writing, the date is no help, either. The screeching sound of the railway pulls me away from the woman in the cream-colored dress in the picture, and I hurry to get into the metro car.

"I think it's Italian," Natasha, my childhood friend and roommate, says as we sit in the university cafeteria, drinking coffee. "Where did you get this photo? It's old." She turns it over and over, looking at the woman.

"I just found it. It's not important." I take the photo from her and put it back in my pocket.

"Wait, let me look again." She reaches out and I hand it to her, she examines it again.

"Wait here," she stands up and snatches the picture. Then she disappears down the hall before I manage to stop her, leaving me all alone at the small table with two cups of coffee and a stack of chemistry books.

I lean back on the plastic chair, grab a cigarette from my jacket pocket, and light it with my silver lighter. I shouldn't have let her leave with my photo.

After some time, she returns and places it on the Formica table.

"I couldn't find anyone who speaks Italian, but they said it wasn't a Russian motorcycle," she announces as she sits down beside me.

"Who are they?"

"I found two motorcycle enthusiasts in the mechanical engineering faculty; their whole room is covered with machine blueprints. They said it was an old motorcycle, it dates back even before WWII, maybe German or Italian." She picks up the photo again and turns it over. "It makes sense considering the year."

"I also think it's Italian," I take the photo from Natasha and examine the writing again.

"Where's this photo from?" She lights a cigarette and looks at me.

"I found it at Grandma Mariusha's in an old wooden box with all kinds of medals from the Great Patriotic War."

"Did your grandmother fight in the Great Patriotic War?"

She laughs. "The grandma of the sweet *Oludashkis*?"

"She never talked about it," I reply awkwardly. Ever since we were little girls, Natasha used to come with me to grandma's small apartment after we'd play in the garden. We'd patiently waited in her tiny kitchen for the sweet pancakes she'd serve us.

"Did she tell you who that woman is? It doesn't look like her."

"That's not her in the photo, but she didn't tell me about the woman in it." I try to closely examine the photo, looking at the woman's curly dark hair.

"Maybe grandma Mariusha was in Germany or Italy before the war."

"I don't think she's ever traveled outside of Russia or Ukraine," I reply. "She would have told me about it, although she doesn't usually tell much." I light myself another cigarette.

"This photo must be important to her if she keeps it with the war medals." Natasha smiles at me and blows smoke into the air.

"Grandma, it's me," I knock on the gray wooden door the very next day. Her nosy neighbor gawks at me again from the end of the corridor, but I smile at her and with an indifferent expression, I pull out a cigarette, lighting it right in front of her.

She mutters something about the younger generation and how they no longer respect anyone, and then disappears into her apartment, closing the door behind her.

"Anuchka?" I hear grandma's footsteps behind the wooden door and hurry to put out the cigarette.

"Yes, it's me. How are you?" I smile at her and after she holds her door ajar, she presses me against her large and comforting chest.

"Did your mother send you again?" She heads to the small kitchenette, turning the kettle on.

"Yes," I lie to her. I told Mom I had to stay in my dorms and study for a test.

"She doesn't need to send you over. I can manage on my own." She puts the kettle on the stove and searches for a match.

"Grandma, have you ever been to Germany?" I stand next to her, offering her the matchbox.

"Why would I want to go to Germany?" She stares at me. "I hate the Germans. Hitler's army was sent to kill us." She holds the lit match with a trembling hand and turns on the gas.

"And Italy? Have you been to Italy?"

"Why would I go to Italy? What's wrong with Kyiv?" She blows out the match before taking out the glass teacups that she keeps in the small cabinet above the counter. "Why do you ask?"

"No reason." I feel the picture tucked in my jacket pocket with my fingers. "I thought perhaps you'd gone on a trip to Italy or somewhere else." I want to ask her who Francesca is, but I'm embarrassed. She'll probably be angry because I took the photo.

"Anouchka..." She places the glass cups on the counter as we wait for the water to boil. "Years ago, it was impossible to go to Italy or anywhere else. It's nothing like today, when people can hop on a train or a plane and go wherever they want. When the communists were in power, the official of the Soviet party had to provide people with a formal travel permit. We had to explain why and where we were traveling to. We were allowed to leave only if the official permitted us to do so. He'd fill out forms that were later inspected at the train station, confirming you were indeed allowed to buy a train ticket," she sighs. "Without a proper permit, you couldn't go anywhere."

"And before the Great Patriotic War, didn't you want to travel?"

"The Soviets were already here before the Great War. They sent me to work at the large tractor plant in Stalingrad, Russia." She puts the fire out and pours hot water from the kettle into the glasses. "I was a young woman about your age. No one asked what an eighteen-year-old girl wanted to do. They just set a quota of women who had to work for Mother Russia." Her hand trembles as she gently stirs the tea. "But that was a long time ago. Thank God Stalin is dead," she smiles at me

"Thanks." I hold the hot teacup and blow on it.

"You know, Anuchka," she smiles at me as we sit on the small floral couch in her living room. "Once, many years ago, after the war was over, when I returned to my childhood's collective farm, I thought about Italy and Rome. But it was an exceptionally long time ago. I had to work on the farm and find a nice husband. It's very different nowadays." She sips her tea, unbothered by the heat of the liquid.

I want to ask her why she mentioned Italy and Rome, but I'm too embarrassed. We continue sipping our tea in silence. If she falls asleep again, I'll put the photo of the woman standing next to the motorcycle back in the wooden box.

The White Dress
November 1940, Rome, Italy

Francesca

"Francesca, please smile," he says to me, but I look away. I shouldn't have let him bring me to this city.

The square around us is crowded as people look at the magnificent sculptures, talk loudly, and take pictures of the marble fountains and the surrounding buildings.

"Francesca," he asks me again, but I stand put next to the motorcycle and refuse to look at him, not wanting him to see my tears. There are several soldiers in the crowd hugging their girlfriends tightly, as if they want to take a mental snapshot of their trip to Rome.

"Francesca, what's wrong?" I hear his voice over the vehicles driving around the square, honking on the busy road. He's a few steps away, holding a camera and pointing it in my direction. I shouldn't have come to Rome with him. I shouldn't have met him again. I shouldn't have told him my name.

A couple of days after he had visited me at the village, he came again. We walked in the fields around, strolled between old cypress avenues and talked. He kept coming, repeatedly, trying to convince me to come with him to Rome. So, we've been roaming the streets of the city since the morning. He showed me the city's narrow streets and magnificent squares and sculptures surrounded by enamored couples. I hugged him as we rode his motorcycle and looked away each time we drove past a policeman or a Blackshirt, afraid that they'd somehow recognize me.

"Francesca, smile," he calls to me. Pigeons fly around us, and I see a soldier buying his sweetheart a small bag of corn seeds from the old man standing at the square. The pigeons fly close to her, flapping their wings as she laughs.

"No." I look at the soldier who turns to kiss her. Why does he want to take a picture of me? Will he forget me tomorrow?

"Francesca, I'm taking a picture."

"What are we?" I start walking towards him, and he puts the camera down.

"What do you mean?"

"What are we?" I stare into his dark eyes. When will he turn back and leave me?

Emanuele stops smiling and takes a step forward; I can smell his familiar scent. As we rode the motorcycle all the way here, I closed my eyes as I hugged and smelled him, trying to keep him and the smell of his leather jacket in my memory. I whispered his name over and over, feeling the words roll on my lips.

"You're with me," he says, trying to come closer, but I take a step back.

"We're not together. You're from here, and I'm from there."

"There's no more here and there. We're in the same Italy."

"There's always a here and there, and we're in a fascist Italy at war. Have you forgotten how we met? We'll never be together." I can see out of the corner of my eye the soldier and his sweetheart walking away hand-in-hand.

"You're right," he keeps looking at me. "You're from there, and I'm from here, and maybe there's a war, and maybe we'll never be together." He speaks slowly, and my eyes well up. I look down even though I have to keep looking at him. "But I know one thing," he closes the distance between us and holds me, brings his lips close to mine, and starts kissing me passionately.

At first, I'm taken by surprise, and I push him away from me. But Emanuele holds me tightly as his soft lips touch mine. He kisses me gently, unlike his arms that are firmly wrapped around my body as he strokes my back. I slightly open my mouth, allowing our tongues to touch ever so lightly before I free myself from his arms and slap him across the face.

"What are we?" I look at him and breathe heavily, my whole body is on fire. I take one step away from him and look into his eyes, wanting him to try to kiss me again. Will he leave me after that kiss?

"I only know one thing," he gasps and grabs both of my hands tightly, preventing me from slapping him again. "I know that you're my girl."

"Okay," I smile at him and let him keep his grip on my hands. I like the touch of his hands against mine. "Now you can take my picture."

But when I stand next to his motorcycle, straighten my dress, and look in his direction, I hear something loud coming from the sky. A large formation of Italian military bombers slowly flies over the city. Even though the crowd looks up to the sky and cheers, I make sure to direct my gaze at Emanuele and smile for the camera. All I notice is the airplanes' gray shadow momentarily moving across the square.

A late-October rain washes over the reddish houses in Rome, painting the walls a darker shade on that cloudy afternoon. We're forced to hide from the rain under a small awning on one of the streets.

"Emanuele, stop. I'm not that kind of girl," I push his hand away as he tries to caress my body through my dress, briefly touching my breasts. Although occasionally I am that kind of girl.

"Francesca, I like feeling your beautiful lips," he whispers to me as his hands continue fluttering up my dress, climbing all the way up to my hair and the back of my neck, then bringing our lips together for another kiss.

We've been meeting in Rome every now and then for several months. We walk down the streets and look at the cafés. The war against England that had been declared at the beginning of the summer is hardly ever mentioned in the newspapers or the cinema newsreels. Still, a newspaper boy passes by, announcing that the German Air Force is mercilessly bombing London. The people in the village say that soon England will surrender, and the war will be over. But in the meantime, every time I manage to arrive to Rome to meet with Emanuele, I see that the city has remained the same. The only difference is that the cafés seem to be almost empty.

"Not here," I giggle and drag him into a side alley, ignoring an older man passing us by and looking at us reproachfully. Maybe we'll have some more privacy in the alley, and perhaps even find some shelter from the rain.

Back home, as night falls, I think about his lips touching mine. I blush in the dark, ashamed by the sensation at the bottom of my stomach. But I didn't permit him to touch me down there, not even close. Only married couples are allowed to do such things.

"I like smelling your hair," Emanuele presses me against a building wall in the alley and kisses me again. I slip my hands under his leather jacket and caress his skin, feeling his warm hands touching me through my drenched dress.

I didn't tell anyone about him, not even my mother, even though we've been dating for several months. I know that the village women gossip behind my back every evening we return on his motorcycle from Rome. But I don't care. I quickly say goodbye to him and rush into my house, waiting for the next time we meet. This isn't the time to fall in love, not while we're in war, even if it is far away in London or the African desert.

"Emanuele, no." I gasp and move his palm as it caresses my wet cheek and starts slowly moving from my neck down my dress as I begin to pant.

"We have to go back," he whispers.

"Yes, you should take me back. It's getting late." I break away from the wall and hold his hand. We start walking towards his motorcycle, parked on one of the streets.

The rain keeps falling, and the streets are almost entirely empty, and yet, I notice two workers in blue overalls hanging a new poster on the bulletin board in a small square. I approach and look at the black letters.

"Francesca, come on, we're getting wet." Emanuele tries to pull on my hand, but I keep staying put and reading the letters on the white paper that is now wet with rain. "Francesca, what are you doing?" He comes back and stands next to me.

"No one will join their army," I peel off the wet paper with my fingernails, destroying the black letters announcing a general recruitment of all the men between the ages of eighteen and thirty-five.

"It's dangerous. They have their own policemen on the streets." He tries to grab my hand.

"If Mr. Mussolini wants, he can go to war with Mr. Hitler hand-in-hand. But he won't recruit Italian soldiers." My fingers keep ripping the poster. "Make sure no one is coming."

"That won't make a difference."

"It will. I've already told you that I wasn't going to give up." I look with satisfaction at the torn poster.

"The War Offices who send soldiers into battle always win."

"They beat my dad, but they won't beat me. I won't stop. You can wait for me by the motorcycle." I mustn't think about my father. I'm with Emanuele now.

"What happened to your father?" He stays at my side.

"They just came at night and took him for questioning," I tear off more paper; my eyes well up. "And then they said he had a car accident in Rome and that there would be no police investigation." I kick what's left of the poster with my wet shoes, ignoring the pain.

"I'm so sorry about your dad." His arms wrap around me from behind, hugging me as I continue to destroy the poster, throwing the shreds on the wet pavement.

"They just brought him back in a coffin." Tears run down my cheeks, mixing with the raindrops.

"I'm so sorry," He keeps hugging me and doesn't try to stop me as I continue to destroy the poster until it's completely unreadable.

"At least I can somehow stop them," I wipe my tears with my palm, looking at the paper scraps on the street.

"We can't stop them. It's already too late," he whispers.

"Let's get out of here." I hug him back as we walk down the empty street. Everyone ran away from the rain. I caress his cold fingers resting on my shoulder and try to relax. What did he mean when he said it was too late?

"What did you mean?" I ask him as we continue walking.
"Regarding what?"
"Why did you say it was too late?" I halt. What was he trying to tell me?
"It's too late. They've been sending letters in the mail too," he says quietly, and I feel the weight of his palm on my shoulder.
"What does that mean?" I ask him again and turn to him, pushing my wet black hair out of my eyes. His eyes are red with tears too. What did they send in the mail?
"Never mind, come on." He starts walking towards the motorcycle parked on the other side of the street, covered with a tarpaulin.
"Are you hiding something from me?" I raise my voice.
"They mailed it to me." He stops and turns, his short black hair glistening in the rain.
"Who are they?" I ask, even though I already know the answer.
"They." He gestures with his head at the torn poster on the bulletin board, already far away from us.
"Are they recruiting you?" My temples start to pound. I hear drums of endless soldier parades, like the ones I see in the newsreels at the cinema before the movie starts.
"Yes," he just shakes his head and seems to slouch.
"Take me back to the village," I walk quickly walk past him.

"Francesca, enough! We're at war. We knew it was coming." He tries to grab my hand and stop me.

"Why didn't you tell me? Take me back to my village. It was bad luck that I met you," I shout at him, hitting his chest with my free hand.

"It wasn't bad luck. I'm glad you got on my motorcycle." He holds me tightly. His eyes are wet with tears or rain, I can't tell anymore.

"I shouldn't have, nothing good came of that day. I shouldn't have come to your city. I hate this place!" I scream at him through the tears and raindrops. I pull my hands away from his and walk as fast as I can to the motorcycle, quickly removing the tarpaulin cover then kicking the rubber wheel. But the motorcycle only moves slightly and doesn't fall. I kick it again.

"I'm not taking you back to the village. I'm taking you to meet my family." He grabs the wet tarp from the pavement, puts it back on the motorcycle, covers the seat, and tries to hug me, even though I resist.

"I'm not coming to meet your family. I'm a simple girl from a village south of Rome. They'll never accept me. They're also fascists. You told me that they are," I break away from his embrace again and start walking away. I'll find the bus station. I'll be fine even if I have to wait here all night in the rain. "I don't want to see you anymore," I yell at him, knowing I'll regret it.

"Not if you'll be my wife." I hear him shout and stop in my place. I turn to him. Why did he just say that?

"What did you say?" I look at him through drops and tears.

"Not if you'll be my wife." He approaches me.

"I won't marry you." I gasp. I mustn't marry him. It's bad luck. He's from here, and I'm from there.

"Please, Francesca, we're at war. We don't have time to wait."

"You're with me just to pass the time, and now you're going to war," I shout at him.

"I've loved you since you left me outside the bakery that night and walked proudly in the empty street," he yells back at me.

"I don't love you. You're from Rome."

"You do love me."

"Then propose."

"Come with me," he holds my hand and starts walking towards the main street. I hold his hand, and when the rain gets stronger, we run, in each other's hands. Where is he taking me? Why isn't he proposing to me? "Wait here." He leaves me shivering under a small awning and enters a jewelry store.

"I won't marry you. They'll take you away from me." I cry as he comes out of the store and walks towards me in the rain.

"Francesca Albergo," he kneels before me on the wet pavement. "Will you be my wife?" he offers me a ring.

"Yes, my Emanuele." I lean in and kiss him, pulling him up to his feet and ignoring the ring. He wants to marry me, even though I have a terrible temper, and even though they're going to take him away from me.

"The ring," he whispers to me as I kiss his lips and place my hands on his chest. I don't care about the ring, and I don't care if someone sees us on the street.

"Hail, Mary, please protect our marriage," I hold my hands tightly together and silently pray as I stand in front of the wooden door in the church chamber. Soon I'll reach out for the metal handle and open the door.

Everyone is already waiting inside, sitting on the wooden pews. Emanuele is also waiting for me at the end of the aisle. This is our day. I look down at the rustling white dress. Despite the war and the rationing announced a few months ago, his family found a seamstress to sew this fancy dress, and I had to agree, even though I didn't want to. I wanted to wear my mother's dress, but it was too plain for them. This church is also much bigger than the one we have in the village. I hear the organ playing through the heavy wooden door. I have to go out; everyone is waiting for me.

"Holy Mary, please take care of my father. He's in the heavens now. I yearn to know that he's okay, that I won't let revenge consume me, letting my heart have a place for love." I clasp my hands together as tight as I can.

Breathe, breathe.

Emanuele is my man, I know that, even though we've only known each other a few months. He's the man with whom in a few minutes, I'll tie my fate with forever.

It's time to go. My hand grips the door's heavy metal handle, and I open it and step into the passage. Aside from the organ's melody ringing through the dim space whose vault is filled with paintings of the Virgin Mary and cherubs, all I can hear is the sound of my footsteps and the rustling of my white dress.

Emanuele had warned me that they'd be here too, and I try not to look at the people sitting on his family's side.

"I apologize," he had told me a couple of days ago. "But many of my family members support him and believe he'll turn Italy into an empire. I must invite them. Otherwise, they'll be suspicious."

I had no choice but to agree, and now they're sitting on the wooden pews on the right side among his family members, standing out in their black uniforms, sitting upright. Their eyes are fixed on me, as if examining and trying to read my thoughts about them. At least they've removed their black visors in the house of God and Mary, who protect me in the heavens. I promised myself I wouldn't hate them anymore, and I know my Emanuele is nothing like them. I also know he loves me. I'm marrying him, not his fascist family. I have my own family and my village. My gaze wanders to the left side of the room, to the empty wooden pews.

Only Mom, Cecilia, and some people from the village have arrived. They're smiling at me as I walk down the aisle. Rome was too far for most of the people who live in the village. Since the Duce had sent the army to occupy Greece, there have been fuel rationings, and there are police checkpoints on the roads inspecting passenger IDs, asking for the purpose of their trip and whether it's necessary. But that's not important right now. All I have to think about is him. He's waiting for me at the end of the aisle, dressed in a uniform and smiling at me.

I hate the uniform that replaced the leather jacket he used to wear. His quiff hairstyle was cut short; but I don't care. I knew it would be my fate when I said yes in that alley in Rome, when we promised each other that we wouldn't take a part in this war while the news kept pouring in from the front.

One step after another, I walk down the aisle until I stand facing the priest, next to my Emanuele. I look up for the last time at the Virgin Mary painted on the church's vault. I closely examine how she reaches her hands out in a gentle gesture towards me. The organ has stopped playing, and all I can hear is the guests breathing, and some random coughing.

"Are you ready to exchange your vows?" The priest asks after he blesses us with the cross as we kneel in front of him.

"Yes."

"Yes," I answer quietly and look at Emanuele for a moment. He was given a few days of leave from boot camp. His green-gray uniform is neatly ironed, reminding me of the German soldiers' uniforms that I had seen several times in Rome. At least they haven't arrived in our village. I smile to my Emanuele. In a moment, he'll be my husband. We'll get through this war.

"Please repeat after me," the priest addresses him. "I, Emanuele Morelli, take you, Francesca Albergo, to be my wife. I promise to be true to you in good times and in bad, in sickness and in health. I will love you and honor you all the days of my life."

"I, Emanuele..." He begins to say the sacred words, and I hear drums beating outside on the street, their loud beat penetrates the church's heavy stone walls, breaking through the closed wooden door.

"It's just a military parade for new recruits," the priest whispers, cross still in hand, he smiles at me encouragingly as Emanuele finishes his vows.

"Now, repeat after me," the priest addresses me. "I, Francesca Albergo, take you, Emanuele…" I can still hear the monotonous sound of drums outside the church. The thump of military boots hitting the pavement in a consistent rhythm, as if they had taken a life of their own.

"I, Francesca Albergo, take you, Emanuele Morelli, to be

my husband," I raise my voice, trying to overcome the sound of the trumpets shaking the church's stained-glass windows. "I promise to be true to you in good times and in bad," I speak louder, "I will love you and honor you all the days of my life," I almost shout, down on my knees, looking up at the Virgin Mary. She must be listening to me.

"In the name of the Father, the Son, and the Holy Spirit, I pronounce you husband and wife," the priest says softly. The church is completely silent, now that the parade has passed through, but the sounds of their bootsteps still echo in my head. I should stop thinking about them.

Emanuele's hand touches mine as we stand in front of the priest, and he pulls me closer, kisses me gently and whispers something into my ear. Still, I can't hear his words over the murmurs of the guests behind us, and I close my eyes and try to surrender to the gentle touch of his lips touching mine. He's my husband from now and forever. I hug his shoulders, stroking the coarse uniform's fabric, feeling his arms wrap around me tightly as we turn to look at the guests who have stood up and smile at us.

As if by order, his Blackshirt family members put on their visors imprinted with the fascist party's symbol and head to the exit. They leave together, rolling out like a pile of coal amidst the women dressed in fancy attire.

"Hello, my wife," he whispers to me.

"Hello, my forever-husband," I answer and smile at him through my tears.

We walk slowly down the aisle, as the guests watch us on both sides. I smile at the older women of his family, all dressed in black, whispering at me as I ignore their cold looks. I don't care. My hand is in Emanuele's as we stand at the center of the church, and the benedictions above our heads surround us.

"Shall we go? They're waiting for us outside," he finally says, and we walk across the emptying church towards the large wooden door and the bright light outside.

"Long live the Duce." We're greeted with a roar the very moment we walk through the doorway and step on the marble steps leading down the street.

In our honor, his Blackshirt family members stand in a two-column formation, facing each other and marking the path outside the church. They saluted Sieg Heil, creating a lane for us to pass through under their raised hands, as the other guests stand behind them and applaud.

Breathe, breathe, don't scream.

My hand tightens around Emanuele's, who stops walking and looks at me.

"Come with me, my beautiful wife," he whispers and leads me down the marble steps towards the saluting Blackshirts.

The autumn sun momentarily emerges from between the clouds, shining down on us as Emanuele quickly pulls me after him between the column of raised hands. As we walk under their Nazi salute, we slouch so as not to touch them and the black fabric of their uniform. I try to look ahead, noticing the black shadow passing over my husband's beautiful face as he passes under them. One, after another, and another.

"Don't say a thing," he whispers and pulls me to the end of the Blackshirt row. "We'll be out of here in just a second."

"Long live our future democratic Italy," I shout as soon as we walk past the last one of them. I stand and salute, feeling the saliva splatter from my mouth at an older, gray-haired, Blackshirt, decorated family member of his. They won't break my spirit.

"Francesca, what are you doing? Come on," Emanuele

pulls me to the motorcycle awaiting us at the end of the street. He clutches my hand and drags me away in front of his astonished family members.

Only when we start driving down the streets, and I hug him tightly, feeling his coarse uniform, do I breathe again and let the wind blow through my hair, as I try to overcome my nausea and the urge to vomit.

Storm Clouds
Italy, June 20, 1941

A summer morning sun seeps through my small bedroom window, and I lie on my bed, look up at the wooden ceiling, careful not to wake my husband.

He's been my husband for several months, but during that time, I've seen him only twelve days. When he wasn't with me, he was away at bootcamp south of Naples. Sometimes he would come for a day or two and then leave again, as I yearned for the touch of his hands.

I lift the blanket a little and look at his tanned skin and toned body from weeks of training in the sun. I examine the abrasion on his right shoulder caused by his rifle's sling.

He moves slightly, and I fight the urge to stroke his back and wake him up, hug his body as I did last night. But I want him to sleep a little longer. He needs to regain strength. Tomorrow, he'll be leaving me again, only this time to another destination. His training period is over. We have one more day left together.

His ironed uniform is neatly laid on a wooden chair at the side of the room. His green coat was hung on the chair's back post, his sergeant ranks displayed proudly. A son of a renowned family from Rome cannot merely be a simple soldier. His excessively polished black army shoes await him at the feet of the chair.

"What are you doing, my beautiful woman?" I hear him whisper and feel his hand stroking my back.

"Touching you," I laugh and cover us both with a thin woolen blanket, lie down on top of him and start moving in slow movements.

When I wake up again and remove the blanket, I find Emanuele standing next to the chair, quietly tucking his uniform's shirt into his pants.

"You're up," he says, and I smile.

"Where are we going?" I sit up in bed.

"To Rome, to visit my family."

"Give me a few minutes, I'll get ready." I stand up and turn to the small wooden cabinet placed against the bedroom wall. I'll choose my prettiest dress.

"Francesca, they asked me to come alone."

"Why?" I shut the closet door and turn to him. I don't think I'll be needing to choose a dress.

"Please, don't be offended, they're not used to you quite yet. They're old fashioned." He approaches me and I take a step back.

"I'm not offended."

"Please, Francesca. I'll be back in the evening. Give them some time to get to know you," he finishes buttoning his shirt and approaches me again.

"No problem," I quickly put on my simple house dress, walk past him, peck him on the cheek and head to the kitchen.

"What are you doing?" He asks me from the bedroom.

"I'll make you some coffee before you head out." I slam the kitchen drawer, ignoring several spoons that had fallen on the stone floor.

"Francesca?"

"We need wood for the oven. I'll go outside to get some." I leave the house, slamming the wooden door behind me. I quickly walk down the stone steps and into the small street. I can feel the smooth, cool touch of the pavement cobblestones. I didn't bother putting shoes on when I rushed out of the house.

All it takes are a couple of steps to reach his ugly motorcycle, which is parked on the street, leaning against the house wall. Using a knife, I stab the front tire with one fierce motion.

The air leaving the tire sounds like a hissing snake. I thrust the knife into the tire, repeatedly, piercing it, slashing through it.

"Francesca, what are you doing?" He shouts, and the wooden door loudly shuts behind him.

"Now they'll know that your wife is crazy!" I keep slicing the tire. "I've had a husband for twelve days, and they've had you for years. If they take issue with a simple village girl, now they'll know she's crazy too." I face him.

"How on earth will I get a new tire when there's a war going on?!" He shouts at me, and I turn my back to him, reaching out for the motorcycle's rear tire.

"I can arrange for a donkey to take you to Rome and back," I reply and raise the knife in my hand, preparing to rip the rear tire as well. However, he grabs me tightly from behind and pushes me away from his motorcycle. "Come on, go to Rome, go to your fascist family, show them your beautiful uniform," I shout and try to break free from his embrace.

"Enough already, my beautiful wife," he holds me tightly and whispers in my ear. "I hate the fascists just as much as you do."

"You're ashamed of me. We shouldn't have gotten married. You should have found a rich girl who's happy to Sieg Heil!" I try to claw his fingers and free myself.

"I'm sorry that I didn't insist on bringing you with me. I was wrong. You're my wife. Forever. I'm proud to be your husband." He plants small kisses on the back of my neck and continues to hug me tightly, keeping me away from his red motorcycle. Why am I so crazy?

"I'm sorry." I wipe my tears and take a deep breath, no longer trying to free myself from his hands that are wrapped around me. I feel the warmth of his body against my back. "Go to Rome. I'll wait here." Why can't I be a quiet woman that men like?

"Even if I want to go, I can't anymore. I want to take you with me," he slowly releases his grip around me, and I drop the knife, hearing the metal blade hit the pavement.

"Let's go find a gas station or a garage. They might have a tire for your motorcycle." I walk slowly up the stairs and back into the house. I need to put my shoes on.

"Your motorcycle, not mine." He says and I turn around. "What?"

"From now on, the motorcycle is yours," he looks at me.

"I don't want it. It's yours."

"I'm leaving it here. You're my wife. I want you to keep it while I'm gone." He climbs up the stairs and stands in front of me.

"I don't know how to ride it."

"I'll teach you," he hugs me again. "We'll find a tire, and I'll teach you to drive."

"I'm really sorry," I whisper. "You have to visit your fascist family in Rome. Give me a minute to put my shoes on."

"Sorry, I don't have that kind of tire," says the gas station worker at the village's outskirts in response to Emanuele presenting him with the torn tire. "What happened to it?" He pokes the ruined tire with his greased fingers.

"We didn't notice there was a knife on the road," Emanuele answers, his hand in mine. *I shouldn't have done it.*

"I don't get any new tires. The government sends all of them to the army." He hands Emanuele the tattered tire. "Try one of the farms outside the village, maybe someone has an old motorcycle."

We thank him and walk away, heading down the path leading outside the village and to the hills.

Hours later, we stop to rest under an oak tree. We've already been to several farms, and no one had a tire. We lie down for a few minutes in the shade, and I place my hand on his chest, feeling his breaths rise and fall. Tomorrow, he'll leave me again.

"Where did you get this harmonica?" I pull a simple harmonica out of his shirt pocket.

"It's been mine since I was a teenager," he says. His eyes are shut, and a blade of hay protrudes from his mouth.

"Can you play it?"

"Just one tune." He smiles, he's eyes still closed, as though he's dreaming.

"Will you play it for me?" I sit on him.

"No," he laughs and rises to kiss me.

"Why not?" I try to resist his kiss.

"Because I only play it when I'm sad." He manages to press his lips against mine. "And since I've met you, I haven't been sad."

"You married a crazy woman." I kiss him back. "I apologize for having ruined your tire and preventing you from saying goodbye to your rich family." His hands start caressing my body.

Later, we lie on the weeds and watch a flock of birds landing in the nearby field. We must get up and keep looking for a tire.

"Take my harmonica. Keep it until I return." He hands it to me.

"Go away!" I stand up and start chasing the birds in the field. "Fly off," I shout and throw stones at them. The birds quickly spread their wings and take flight, disappearing behind the grove of olive trees on the hill.

"Francesca, what are you doing?" He sits back down and watches me.

"I can't stand just how perfect everything seems," I walk through the empty field among the yellow stalks of grain, wiping tears from my eyes. "This pleasant breeze, the silence, the birds all around, and the two of us lying here under the oak tree; all while knowing that you're leaving me tomorrow." I approach and stand over him. "It's too pleasant for me, and I can't stop thinking when will it end?" My tears continue pouring. I don't care if he sees me cry.

"It won't come to an end." He stands up and hugs me, but we both know he's lying.

"Let's get out of here." I feign a smile and hug him back. "I don't want your harmonica. Keep it for the times you think of me." I kiss him and promise myself I won't ruin the last couple of hours we have left together.

We manage to find a new tire only around evening time, and the village is completely dark when we arrive at my house.

"It's okay, my Francesca. I'll teach you to drive the motorcycle on my next vacation." He places the new tire next to the red motorcycle, still leaning on the stone wall of my house.

"Now I know for sure you'll come back," I say and hold his hand as we climb up the stairs. Tomorrow he'll be gone.

I promised myself I wouldn't cry, and I won't. The next day I hold his hand tightly as we walk towards the village's small train station.

We walk down the main street and past two trucks and a horse pulling a wagon, yet still somewhat far away from the station, I hear trumpets and drums. And as we get closer, I see an orchestra on the side of the platform standing in straight rows.

They're dressed in their festive uniforms and playing a military march. The conductor stands there with his back to us and vigorously instructs the musicians, enthusiastically waving his hands. Fascist party flags were hung on the small station building next to the Nazi Germany flags, our ally in the war.

"Read the latest news," shouts the newsboy, waving a newspaper, standing under a red flag with a white circle and a black swastika in its center. His voice is drowned out in the orchestra's commotion.

"Let's go," Emanuele says and holds my hand tightly as we walk to the station, approaching the soldiers who have already arrived. They flood the platform with their green uniforms and duffle bags, hugging and kissing their sweethearts. I notice Cecilia among them, embraced by her new husband. He was also drafted. Recently, there have been many weddings in the village. All the women around us are hugging their beloved soldiers as if trying to stop time before they board the train awaiting them.

The train is already at the station, and the passenger car doors are wide open. One by one, the soldiers begin walking in, laughing, and kissing their girls, possibly for the last time.

"Take it with you," I say to Emanuele and put a photo in his hand. It's the one he had taken that time in Rome when I stood next to his motorcycle. "So, you have something to remember me by."

"I'll never forget you." He hugs me tightly, and I wrap my arms around him, touching his rigid uniform and large duffle bag.

"Don't do it. It's dangerous, don't get into the monster," I hear someone shouting and turn my head. I spot Crazy Gabriele running down the platform dressed in his dirty military coat. He tries to pull the soldiers away from the cars and the black locomotive smoking thick whiffs of steam. "Get out! The monster will eat you," he shouts to a soldier who's about to enter the car. He waves his hands in the soldier's face, blocking his way. But the soldier laughs at him and slaps Crazy Gabriele.

"Ignore him. He's sick," I stop hugging Emanuele and shout at the soldier. I start walking in his direction.

"Who is he?" Emanuele asks as he follows me.

"Our village madman," I answer as we approach Gabriele. "He's been like that ever since I was a young girl."

But a group of soldiers gather around him, mocking, knocking his hat off as he tried running away from them while waving his hands.

"Don't get on the train. It's black," he shouts past me over the sound of the soldiers' laughter. I follow him with my gaze as he runs down the platform and reaches the station building. He starts tearing the Nazi flag down. "The red cape wakes the monster. The red cape wakes the monster!" He shouts as he unsuccessfully tries to pull on the Nazi flag.

"Gabriele, stop!" I shout to him from a distance and start walking in his direction. But before I do, two policemen approach and beat him, forcefully kicking him down.

"Leave him alone," Emanuele tries to grab my hand, but I break free from and run towards the policemen, pushing one of them back and standing over Gabriele, gasping. I don't know those policemen.

"Who are you?" One of them grips my arm and shoves me against the building wall.

"She's with me. Leave her at once." I hear Emanuele's voice.

"She mustn't interfere with police work," the policeman replies and continues to hold me tightly, pinning me against the stone wall. My chest, forces against the hard stone, burns as I struggle to breathe. The policeman pinches the back of my neck.

"Let go of her. Immediately. Attention, soldier!" My husband's voice booms, and the policeman's sweaty fingers slowly release their grip on me.

"She disturbed us, Sergeant." I turn around and look at the policeman standing in attention in front of Emanuele.

"Your police work is over. Unhand them," Emanuele says as I slowly catch my breath, trying to shake off the feeling of his fingers touching the back of my neck.

"Yes, Sergeant," he says and starts walking away. I look at the other policeman who stayed behind. My husband stands between him and me until the policeman gives in and leaves too.

"We must destroy the monster. Seeing red everywhere hurts my eyes," Crazy Gabriele mumbles still on the floor. There's a trickle of blood dripping down his nose, his eyes are closed.

"The monster will leave soon enough," I say to him as tears roll down his cheeks. I need to help him, but I have to go. I must say goodbye to my husband. The soldiers have started boarding the train.

"Take it," Emanuele pulls a clean handkerchief from his uniform pocket. He kneels and places it in Gabriele's filthy hand. "Your nose is bleeding."

Gabriele momentarily opens his eyes and looks at my husband. "I have the same uniform," he says and closes his eyes again, curled up on the platform floor.

"I'm sorry," I hold my Emanuele's hand, and we walk away. "He's the village madman. Surely there are crazy men in Rome."

"Francesca Morelli, I don't think I've ever heard you apologize." He laughs and pulls me closer, kissing my lips. "Don't make a habit of it. And there are no madmen in Rome, only men who think they can rule the world."

"All aboard," the conductor calls out and blows his whistle. The orchestra increases the military march's tempo. Surrounded by the soldiers swarming the train, I hug and kiss him once more as hard as I can.

"Take care," I say and briefly hold his hand peeking from the window. He reaches both arms out and hugs me. I stand on my tiptoes to reach him.

"I'll be back soon," he whispers when we hear the locomotive's whistling.

"If something happens to you, I'll come to rescue you." I start walking by his car as the train starts moving.

"Nothing will happen to me, I promise." He grasps my hand, and I'm forced to start running as I sense his warm fingers on mine.

"Promise you'll come back?" I continue running, holding him for another second.

"Francesca Morelli, nothing will stop me from returning to you," he shouts when our hands are separated.

"I'm waiting for you. Just come back to me!" I cry out. I stop running and try to catch my breath, watching the train grow smaller and smaller as does his image and arm waving goodbye. The train leaves a black cloud in the sky.

Only after the train disappears behind the hills and the black smoke dissipates in the morning breeze do I turn around and start walking back.

The station is silent again. Most women and attendants have already left the station. They all walk past Crazy Gabriele, whose eyes are still shut, and his body curled in a fetal position. Even the orchestra players start putting away their drums and trumpets.

"This morning, the German army launched an attack on the Soviet Union," the newsboy announces. He walks among the remaining musicians and waves the newspaper over his head. "Read it, Mussolini congratulates Hitler on the war against the Bolsheviks and offers his assistance."

My Francesca. I hold the letter that arrived in the mail a couple of days ago.

We are in a peaceful and quiet place, and sometimes I can imagine that the war that tore us apart doesn't exist at all. I can't tell you where I am. Still, I can write that we are surrounded by tall mountains covered in snow that piled up before the winter, and the trees and lakes around our camp seem to have been taken from a fairyland. Thank God that for us the war is nothing but a headline on a newspaper, which we occasionally receive, and the boring obligatory lookouts. But I use all my free time to think about you and your smile. I miss you so much.

I slowly walk down the alley towards the village square. I'm dressed in my woolen coat to protect me from the cold and am careful not to slip on the pavement that's still we from last night's rain. It's been six months since he boarded the train on that summer day, and everything has changed.

Winter winds have replaced the warm summer breeze, and Christmas this year is modest. The fir tree in our cold house is almost bare of decorations, and the streets weren't decorated with twinkly lights as they were in previous years. To make matters worse, the food allowance at the village grocery store is dwindling, even though I need to eat more. I'm eating for two.

I smile and caress my swollen belly through the woolen dress. I can feel her kicking, like a gentle flutter inside. I know she's a girl. Holy Mary whispered to me that I'll have a daughter. But I haven't written to him about it yet. I don't want him to worry when he's so far away.

Down the alley, I notice a new Fascist poster on the bulletin board. It features a heroic soldier wearing a helmet and holding a rifle, storming the enemy. For a moment, I stop and pretend to look at the poster. Then, I gently remove my gloves and intend to peel the poster off. However, in a brief second, I change my mind and keep walking. Even though the policemen probably don't patrol the streets during such a cold weather, I can't take any risk.

I haven't seen Crazy Gabriele recently. He must be hiding somewhere from the cold. I saw him once huddled inside the small shed where I had hidden the motorcycle. But when I tried to approach him, he started crying and ran away.

I couldn't replace the motorcycle's tire. When winter broke, I had to push it into the old shed next to our house, cover it with a tarp and hide it beside the woodpile. Luckily, I did it a few months ago when I didn't know I was pregnant. Now I was no longer able to strain myself. Sometimes, soldiers come to the village and confiscate horses, sending them to the Italian army fighting in Russia. They also take donkeys and send them overseas to the soldiers in North Africa. At the beginning of winter, the newspapers boasted the names of cities that the Germans had conquered in Russia - Minsk, Kyiv, Odesa. The headlines declared that the Russians were about to surrender, but since Christmas, the papers hadn't mentioned the matter, and according to rumors the Germans were at Moscow's outskirts and retreating due to the heavy snow and the Russians' attack. Is Emanuele telling me the truth; he isn't fighting? I don't want him to fight anyone, and I don't want him to conquer any city. I just want him to come back to me.

"Daddy will be home soon," I whisper to the baby in my belly as I carefully walk up the church stairs.

"Saint Mary," I kneel before her statue, cross myself and look down. "Please bring Emanuele safely back home and end this silly war. Please give me a daughter, not a son, so he'll never have to fight." I stop for a moment and caress my bump, knowing that she's listening. "Holy Mary…" I shut my eyes, but then open them when I hear a rustling noise nearby.

Cecilia slowly approaches me, pacing between the pews. She kneels beside me, smiles faintly, turns to the Holy Virgin, crosses herself, and starts praying.

"Holy Mary," I close my eyes again, clasp my hands tightly and look up. "Please send word from Cecilia's husband, who's on the battlefield. She hasn't heard from him in months."

After I finish, I look at the candle I lit and slowly leave the dark church. I await Cecilia outside. Despite the winter wind, I enjoy standing on the steps overlooking the nearly empty square. The cold air helps relieve my nausea, which I still have from time to time.

"Did he send you another letter?" Cecilia asks when she finally steps out the church, stands next to me, and lights herself a cigarette.

"No," I reply, keeping to myself the fact I've received a letter a couple of days ago.

"Want one?" She offers me a cigarette. But I refuse even though I long for the bitter taste. Smoking makes me nauseous too, and I usually exchange my cigarette allowance at the market for extra food.

"Have you heard from him?" I ask her.

"No," she blows the smoke into the frigid air.

"Maybe you'll get a letter today."

"Yes, maybe I will. Are you heading to the post office?"

"Yes," I slowly walk down the church steps, and cross the square on my way to the post office. Cecilia walks beside me.

The old clerk at the post office is sitting with his back to us, observing the paper strips emerging from the telegraph machine with jarring ticking. Then he reads the text, writes it down on a note, places it into an envelope, and hands the sealed envelope to the boy waiting by his desk. "The Leto family, do you know where they live?"

"Sì," the boy says and holds the envelope tightly in both hands.

"Go, quick." He lightly pats the boy on the back of the head, and the latter runs out. I follow him with my gaze, see him crossing the square and disappearing into one of the alleys.

"Francesca, Cecilia, how are you? Come closer." He smiles at us and walks to the mailbag leaning against a side wall. He sighs, then picks up the canvas sack and pours its contents onto the wooden table behind the counter. When I was a child, he'd give me a paper with a stamp, and whisper that I should picture someone sent me a letter from a faraway land. However, now, he stands before me, white-haired, hunched over, searching through the pile of letters, looking for ours.

As we wait, I look at the board hanging on the wall and telegrams' words are counted. There's a black phone under the board, and a poster with names of countries and the cost of calling each one of them. England, Egypt, Palestine, and the United States were crossed out with a thick red marker. These are enemy states.

"There's one," he says as if to himself and puts it aside. He continues going through the letters. Cecilia and I get a little closer to the counter and try to identify the handwriting, but it's hard to decipher from where we're standing.

The telegraph machine starts ticking again, spewing a new strip of paper. But the clerk keeps scanning through the letters until he finishes going over the whole pack. Only then does he approach us, places the single letter on the counter, and turns again to the noisy machine.

"This one's for you," Cecilia hands me the envelope after having snatched it from his outstretched hand.

"I'm sorry," I say to her and put it in my coat's pocket. I'll read it later when I'm alone.

"It's okay," she leaves of the small post office.

"Cecilia, wait, let's have some coffee." I go after her and try to walk as fast as I can. My belly's getting too big for my own comfort.

"Surely you'll receive a letter from him tomorrow or the day after, or in a week –"

"Or maybe not at all," she blurts as she walks away.

"Surely, you'll get a letter. It's just being delayed."

"You know," she stops and faces me, "North Africa, Libya, or Egypt, or wherever he was sent to fight the Brits, isn't that far from here. There's just a nasty, ugly desert and a small part of the Mediterranean Sea to cross back home. How long do you think it takes for a letter to arrive?"

"He's fine." I place my hand on her arm. "He's fighting a war. Things happen during wartime, and letters are delayed."

"Yes, things happen during wartime." She ignores my hand on hers, turns around, and continues walking to the café in the square. "Some husbands are sent on vacation in the mountains, doing nothing but watch duties because they're sergeants, and other husbands are sent to fight a real war against the English enemy in the desert."

I don't respond and sit down next to her at one of the café tables. Even though it's a late morning hour, the café is almost empty. Except for us, there's a pair of old men sitting at one of the tables and playing chess. The café owner sits next to them and looks at the wooden chess board and the pieces. He doesn't even bother to get up and greet us. In any case, he has nothing to offer us. He hasn't received a coffee delivery from Rome in a long time, and the cake display that was once full of pastries is now empty.

"Hitler can't handle the Russian winter," one of the players says as he moves the white queen.

"Hitler won't give up," his opponent replies and moves his black knight. "Winter will end, and he'll attack again."

"We took the North African desert. The Brits surrendered in Tobruk," the café owner agrees. "We win when it isn't winter."

"Do you think my husband is okay?" Cecilia lights herself another cigarette and asks me after we sit in silence for some time and watch them play.

"I'm sure he's fine." Once again, I put my hand on hers, which is placed on the table. "You heard them," I try to smile at her and glance at the older men playing chess. "They're in the desert and winning, even if you haven't received any letters."

"At least I didn't get any government telegram telling me it's time to throw on a black dress," she smiles and wipes away a tear.

"Don't worry, you won't receive such a telegram. The only letter you'll get is from him." I rub her hand and stay put, even though I want to go home and read Emanuele's love letter.

"At least I'm not pregnant. If I'm going to be a widow, it's better to be childless." She takes a drag and directs her gaze at the two men and the café owner, still playing chess and analyzing the war.

"Yes, if you're going to be a widow, it's best not having children," I reply, as my daughter gently kicks inside. In a couple of months, I'll hold her for the first time and kiss her.

"I can't do it anymore," I scream and bite the piece of cloth that the midwife had shoved into my hand when it all started hours ago. "Get out..." I cry as I had another contraction. I sweat heavily, dampening my rolled-up dress as I lie with my legs spread apart on the bed in my tiny bedroom and shriek in pain.

"Push now, now," the midwife says, firmly holding my legs apart.

"I can't..." I cry out again and shut my eyes, feeling the wetness between my legs. My nails sink deep into the neighbor's hand holding on to me. She's also sweating in the summer's heat.

"Francesca, just a few more pushes," my mother whispers as she wipes my forehead with a cold cloth. "A couple more..."

"Please, get out..." I howl.

"You're okay, push again," the midwife instructs. "Go get more water and find a handfan," I think I hear her saying. Perhaps she said it to the young girl who came in earlier, stood by the door, and looked at me with a terrified look. But I'm not sure anymore.

Breathe, breathe, breathe.

I've been lying on the bed for hours, screaming with every contraction. *Why won't she get out? Where's the doctor?*

"Come on, push. Don't stop now," the midwife encourages me as another wave of pain washes over me, and I whimper and grunt.

"Is she okay?" I think it's my mother asking.

"She's perfectly fine, just keep pushing and don't give up." The midwife peers down between my legs, forcing them open.

"The crazy man outside said that they couldn't cross the checkpoint in the neighboring village so they couldn't get him," the girl says when she reenters the room holding a bucket of water and some newspapers. Frightened, she looks at me again and I start to cry. The village doctor was drafted into the army months ago, and now there's no other doctor. *Why won't she come out*? I violently grip the neighbor's hand again as she wipes my belly with a cold cloth.

"Enough, get her out!" I scream. The whole room seems to be spinning around me in a cacophony of voices, pain, sweat and instructions to push. Someone fans a newspaper in my face. There's more screaming, maybe mine; the bed gets moister between my legs; I stare at the peeling ceiling; someone's hands forcefully open my legs; I yell, scream, and moan. There's yet another contraction, and I sweat even more. Suddenly, everything is silent, and all I can hear, or feel is the air from the makeshift handfan. I breathe and try to raise my head, and silence. Is everything okay?

Then, I hear small whimper, but a whimper, nonetheless. I cry. It hurts so much, but I no longer care about the pain or the hands caressing me. My mother smiles at me, and the girl by the door also smiles embarrassedly as she takes a couple of steps towards me.

"It's a boy," someone says nestles a warm, wet baby on my stomach. He moves as he weeps, and my arms embrace him, touching the blanket he was wrapped in. He's so delicate and small, and he's mine, ours. Mine and my husband's who'll arrive any time soon.

"She should rest," I hear someone whispering, then a

couple of random hands take my son from me, and the door closes quietly. I lie on my side, momentarily looking at the peeling wall, the reddish terra cotta floor, and the wet pieces of cloth scattered around the room.

But before I close my eyes, I read the headlines on the newspaper that was earlier used to cool me down. 'The Germans Launched a New Attack on the Soviet Union. Mussolini will send Italian Reinforcement.'

The Headline
September 2021, Kyiv, Ukraine

Anna

"Anuchka, more cherry piroshki?" Grandma holds out the plate laden with small pastries and offers me one. I smile at her, take another one and bite the sweet pastry sprinkled with snow-like sugar. She bends over and places the plate on the coffee table. I search for an excuse to ask her more questions.

"Did you read the newspaper?" I grab the paper on the couch. The big red headlines announce a looming invasion.

"About the Russians? That they want to invade us?" She gets up and heads to the kitchen. She's probably getting something else for me to eat.

"Yes," I say, looking at the colorful photograph of a Russian tank procession in Moscow's Red Square. "Back in the war, were you as worried as you are today?"

"In the Great Patriotic War?" She asks from the kitchen.

"Yes." I should tell her that I took the old photo, the one that I didn't have time to return.

"When the war started and the Nazis invaded, we didn't know what was going on. We didn't have a TV or cell phones to keep us updated at all times." I can hear her opening the refrigerator. "Back then, all the newspapers belonged to the government. They only printed what they wanted us to know." She briefly steps into the living room and puts a jar of jam on the table before she returns to the small kitchen.

"Thanks," I say and follow her to the kitchen to see if she needs any help, but mostly so I can keep listening to her.

"Back then," grandma keeps talking, "we worked eighteen-hour shifts at the big tractor plant in Stalingrad. There was a huge poster of Stalin, the 'Father of Nations,' on the factory wall." She says contemptuously, "the party's political leaders said that we were defeating the German invaders." She stops talking for a moment. "They said we shouldn't spread rumors that we were losing, but we started assembling tanks instead of tractors. The whole city was covered in sandbags against aerial bombing, and we still believed that the Germans wouldn't come."

"And did they?" I take another bite of the sweet piroshki. Where did she get that old photo? The same photo tucked in my coat pocket.

"One day they arrived," she sighs. "It was a quiet Sunday afternoon. It was summer and I remember warm sun in the streets." She smiles at me as she starts washing the dishes. "Suddenly, they flew over the city like a huge flock of black birds darkening the blue skies. That day, the whole city was bombed and burning. After that day, we stopped believing the party's political leaders, who claimed that we were winning, and everything was fine." She goes to the living room and grabs the empty piroshki plate.

"Do you think they'll invade us? Will they actually do it?" I follow her and take another look at the photo in the newspaper, featuring the Russian tanks and their cannons facing the photographer.

"I don't know." She stops doing the dishes. "But I know one thing," she looks at me, "I don't believe leaders and decorated generals hiding in their fancy bunkers. They don't care about us. We, the women at home, are always those who pay the price and are last to know."

A Quiet Eastern Front
Italy, Autumn, 1942,
A Couple of Months After the Outbreak of the German Summer Offensive in Russia

Francesca

"I'm sorry, Francesca, there's no letter today." The old post office clerk smiles at me sadly and makes funny sounds at Raffaele, who's in my arms. Raffaele is wrapped in a soft blanket and a woolen hat, he's asleep and dreaming his baby dreams. He doesn't know that I haven't received a sign of life from his father in months. Why didn't I tell him that I was pregnant?

"Thanks." I peek behind his shoulder to see if there might be a mailbag he forgot to open. But the wooden table at the back of the office is empty.

"The newspapers say we beat the Russians in Stalingrad," he smiles encouragingly.

"Yes, that's what the paper says." I smile at him bitterly, and stroke Raffaele's head. Neither of us believe the newspapers.

"If something comes up, I promise I'll let you know," he says, ignoring the teleprinter that starts ticking monotonously and ejecting a paper strip.

"Thank you," I head for the exit. I don't want the telegram boy appearing at my front door, handing me a sealed envelope with an apologetic look, and then hurrying off before I can open it. I see him, every now and then, rushing along the small streets, and duck into one of the alleys, praying he won't spot me and hand me a folded yellow paper. Anything but a telegram like the one Cecilia received at the height of summer.

"Have a nice day and take care of your cute baby." The old, hunched clerk gets up from his wooden chair and approaches the teleprinter. "Maybe you'll hear something in Rome. Who knows."

"What do you mean?" I stop and turn around.

"Maybe they know something in Rome, and they're keeping it from us," he gestures with his head towards the ticking teleprinter and the paper strip slowly emerging from the machine.

"Thanks," I leave the post office. I'll wait for the letter; it must be on its way.

A pleasant autumn sun shines down on the village square, and I stroke Raffaele's head as I walk past the fountain and the café. When summer started, they'd opened it again, and the coffee and cakes were back. The German soldiers brought the coffee and food from the nearby airport they had recently built beyond the hill.

At first, a couple of German soldiers came in driving in several gray-blue jeeps loaded with equipment. They parked in the village square for a few minutes and looked around before they moved on to the fields behind the hill.

Then came the tractors and the forced laborers they had brought from Poland. They destroyed the ancient olive groves, straightened the fields into a barbed wire camp and runways illuminated at night by watchtowers. Despite the milk I needed for Raffaele, I tried to eat less, and gave some of my food to the laborers who delivered food at night to the people kept behind the barbed wire fences. But now they too have disappeared and were replaced by German bomber planes and German soldiers who regularly visit the village, spending their German money at the local café.

I turn my gaze away from them and start walking home, shoving my hand in my pocket, and feeling for the last letter I've received from him months ago. I've opened and reopened the letter so many times, that the thin paper has nearly ripped. I should have told him I was pregnant when he was still receiving my love notes.

"Francesca!" I hear someone calling my name, and I spot Cecilia sitting in the square at one of the café tables. She's waving at me. I need to sit with her; I can't leave her alone.

"How are you?" I sit on the chair beside her, ignoring the German soldiers at the café.

"I'm fine. And you?" She smiles at me and rumples her black dress. The ashtray on the table is full of cigarette butts.

"I'm fine, too." I caress Raffaele's head.

"Did you get a new letter?" She asks.

"No, perhaps tomorrow."

"You could ask the butcher. He'll probably have something new to tell you." She looks at his shop on the other side of the square.

"It's fine, I'll wait for the letter." I look at his shop too. There's been rumors that he or someone he knows have been listening to the British radio, the BBC, even though it's considered treason.

"Maybe it's better to receive nothing and know nothing." She smiles to herself and lights another cigarette. For the past couple of months, I've been giving her my cigarette allowance instead of selling it on the black market.

"Did they tell you anything else?"

"Other than that telegram?" She looks at two German officers sitting next to us. "No, they don't tell me anything else. All I know is that he was killed in *El Alamein* in Libya or Egypt. What kind of a name is *El Alamein*? What a place to die in!" She blows smoke at the German soldiers, but I don't think they notice.

"Do you think they'll know more in Rome?"

"What could they possibly know there? All they do is send *them* here," she gestures with her head at the German soldiers.

"Perhaps the Ministry of Defense knows something or the Ministry of Propaganda."

"Perhaps the fashion bureau, who provides the black fabric for widows' dresses, or the paper bureau, who supplies the telegram papers, or the ink bureau, the same pitch-black ink they use to write the letters." She puts out her cigarette in the ashtray, even though she's barely smoked it.

"I didn't mean it." I place my hand on hers. "I'm trying to help."

"Do you think you can help me?" She pulls the cigarette pack out. "No one can help me anymore, not even at the government's Ministry of Birth." She sticks another cigarette between her lips.

"May I?" The German officer at the table next to us gets up and reaches out, holding a lighter. Cecilia turns to him.

"Danke," she smiles at him. He smiles back at her and approaches us, looking at me.

"Cute baby," he reaches his hand out and touches Raffaele's head before he returns to sit by the other officer.

"*Danke*." I smile at him politely, fighting my sudden urge to slap him.

"See?" Cecilia smiles at me bitterly. "They do know something in Rome, after all." She blows out smoke. "They know how to send over nice German soldiers to replace the men they'd taken for their war. Maybe we should start taking advantage of what they sent us."

Raffaele starts to cry on the way home, but I ignore his cries and stand next to the billboard, looking at the new poster boosting the village's morale. The poster features an Italian and a German soldier shaking hands as their hobnailed boots stomp on a Russian flag.

"I'm so sorry," I whisper to Raffaele, and rip the poster with my fingernails, destroying the paper while my other hand caresses him, trying to soothe him. "I should have written to him; I should have told him I was pregnant." I throw the torn paper on the ground. "I didn't want to worry him, and now he doesn't even know that you were born." I sit on the pavement, ignoring the dirty stones, and lean against the torn poster, hearing nothing but Raffaele's cries.

"Why did I get on his motorcycle? And why are you crying?" I wipe my teary eyes. "Stop crying. Can't you see this isn't helping? Don't you understand that no one can tell me where your father is? Can't you see we're all alone?" I ignore Raffaele's wailing. *Why isn't he writing to me?*

A man walks down the alley and looks at us, but he doesn't say anything and keeps walking, leaving me alone with Raffaele wrapped in a simple woolen blanket in my arms.

"Eat, my child," I say to him after a while, pulling my breast out to nurse him. I cover his head with the thin blanket and caress his cheek. "Mommy's here. I'll take care of you."

What is that noise? I open my eyes and listen to the rustling sounds. It's dark outside, probably midnight. I quickly reach for the knife I keep under my pillow. I hold the hilt firmly and listen.

Raffaele is sleeping peacefully in his crib; his breathing quiet. Even the small alley in the village is quiet. Where did that noise come from? From the small shed? Is someone trying to steal my winter firewood; the same firewood I had slowly collected over the past couple of months?

"Keep sleeping." I bend over to Raffaele and kiss him gently. I quickly put on a simple dress over my nightgown. I have to protect my firewood; winter is coming.

I creep along barefoot, all the way to the shed. I feel the cold touch of the stones under my feet, but my hand holding the knife is sweating. I need to be quiet. The shed door is open, and I hear someone whispering inside.

"You're a good motorcycle," someone says. "I'll clean you," the stranger continues. "You're a good motorcycle. I'll fix you," he keeps saying.

Breathe, breathe, breathe.

My hand tightens around the hilt, and I open the door wide.

"Don't touch the motorcycle!" I scream and charge the stranger in the dark, pointing my knife at the whispers. *No one's going to take his bike from me.*

"Don't do it. It's dangerous." I hear a whimper in the dark.

"Gabriele?" I gasp and stop. *Did I hurt him?* I don't think I stabbed him.

"Don't do it. It's dangerous," the whining continues.

"Gabriele, are you okay?" I grope for him in the dark. *Where did he go?*

"Gabriele didn't do anything. Gabriele protected the motorcycle," he continues whining in the corner as I fumble around in the dark. Finally, I touch him and feel his tattered woolen coat and shaggy hair.

"Are you okay? Were you hurt?" I ask him, but he just keeps whining. I rush back home and return with a lit lantern and two slices of leftover bread. "Are you okay?" I examine him by the light as he hungrily chews the slices of bread.

"It's too dangerous to ride the motorcycle. They're about to attack," he whispers to himself.

"There's no attack, and this motorcycle is broken. The tire needs to be changed, and I don't know how."

"It's dangerous. They'll shoot me soon. I need to run away."

"There's no war, Gabriele. The war is far away." I want to stroke his dirty, shaggy hair, but I just can't.

"Soon, it's dangerous. They'll shoot me. They're coming," he whispers as he chews the second slice. "It's a good motorcycle. It will take care of you."

"Do you know anything about motorcycles?" *Could he help me?*

"In the previous war..." he starts speaking, then stops.

"What happened there?" I look at him. He looks back at me and holds out his hand. "Do you know how to change a tire?" I approach him and touch his outstretched hand, but he doesn't answer me and just leaves his hand there. "Wait a minute." I hurry home and grab an apple from the kitchen. I return and hand it to him.

"I do." He chews the apple and slowly approaches the tire thrown against the shed wall.

 "Will you change it for me?"

"Gabriele Di Maggio, Fourth Rifle Regiment, Forward Ranger, Third Motorcycle Platoon." He looks at me, and under the dim lantern light, I can see his teary eyes. "It's dangerous. They'll shoot. I need to run away from the fire."

He hugs the tire as he sits on the ground, softly caressing the rubber.

"Gabriele, stay here tonight. Can you take care of the motorcycle for me?" I finally leave him behind and manage to caress his dirty coat for a second. I hope he understood what I meant, and will change the flat tire, but I'm not sure. He stayed seated on the floor, muttering, and hugging the new tire as if he had to cling to something.

Back home, I clean my hands, kiss Raffaele, and go back to sleep, but not before I tuck the knife under my pillow again. Tomorrow, after I'll drop by the post office, I'll try to get him some food. He'll take care of the motorcycle.

"How can I help you?" The soldier standing behind the post office counter asks me the next day. He speaks Italian with a German accent. He's wearing the gray-green German army uniform. I keep silent for a moment and look at the old clerk standing with his back to me, sorting the envelopes on the table. "I'm here to help him," the soldier adds with a smile when he notices my gaze.

"I'll wait," I reply and stand by the wall, crossing my arms on my chest and leaning against the bulletin board.

"As you wish," he says, no longer smiling. He turns around, and heads to the teleprinter. They seemed to have replaced the old machine with a larger one, emblazoned with a large black swastika held in the talons of an eagle, its wings spread out.

"I'm sorry, Francesca, but I don't have a letter for you today." The old clerk smiles at me a few minutes later. He finishes sorting the letters and approaches the counter.

"It's okay," I smile at him, even though I want to scream.

"He's helping me with the mail." He glances at the German soldier who stands with his back to us, or maybe he glimpsed at the new poster, portraying the fascist and Nazi flags together. "You'll probably get a letter tomorrow," he says as usual.

"Thanks." I leave the small office, but after a moment, I walk back inside. The old clerk lifts his head and looks at me. "Is there someone you could ask?" I speak quietly and look at the German soldier who stands with his back to us, fiddling with the noisy teleprinter.

"All I know is what Rome tells me. They don't tell me anything here," he looks at the German soldier pulling the paper strips. He looks at me momentarily, then sits down on the wooden table and starts reading.

"Thank you very much. I'll come tomorrow," I raise my voice and leave the small post office. He's a good man, but he won't help me, and I have to go home and feed Raffaele.

The café in the square is full of German soldiers sitting around the small tables, enjoying the autumn sun. Their gray jeeps are parked right next to them.

I ignore them and pass by the fountain, but before I enter the alley, I turn around and start walking back. I need to know.

"Good morning," I close the glass door behind me.

"Sorry, I don't have any ham," the butcher says in German to the soldier in the gray-green uniform standing in front of him.

"I'll pay you as much as you want," the soldier replies. I stand by the door and watch them.

The display case that was once full of meat is now empty; there are only a couple of ducks hanging over it. They'd probably gone hunting.

"Sorry, there isn't any," the butcher nodded.

"I'll take this one," the soldier points to one of the ducks. The butcher grabs it and wraps the animal in brown parchment paper as the soldier pulls out his wallet and places German bills on the counter.

"Francesca, I'm sorry," he addresses me after the soldier leaves the store and the glass door closes behind him. "I don't have any meat for you, the army takes everything."

"It doesn't matter." I haven't been here in a long time. I don't have enough for meat, as it is. "What do you know?"

"About what?"

"About the war." I look at him.

"I know exactly what you do. I read the newspapers just like you." He stares back.

"That isn't the word on the street."

"What is the word on the street then?" He starts lining up his knives on the counter.

"That you listen to other things, like the BBC. They say that you know things," I say quietly, even though it's just us two here.

"People have big mouths," he starts sharpening one of the knives, smoothing it with swift movements.

"I need to know." I lean in as close as I can, the only thing standing between us is the display case. "Please."

"What do you want to know?" He sighs and glances outside the window at the German soldiers sitting at the café.

"What's going on in Russia?"

"It isn't looking good."

"Don't pity me, please," I clench my fists; my nails dig into my palm.

"They say that the Russians have surrounded the Germans and Italians who are freezing to death in the snow."

"I don't believe you. That's not what the papers say." I spread my hands on the display case. He's lying.

"You can believe whatever you want, the government papers, the posters on the bulletin boards, the fascist radio broadcasting from Rome. You can believe anyone you like." He sighs and places the sharpened knife in a wooden drawer.

"I'll go to Rome and find out." I face the door. He's wrong. My letters are just being delayed.

"Can you get to Rome?"

"No, but I'll find a way." I turn back to him.

"If you do, come see me. Maybe I can help you."

"I'll find a way," I reply and leave his shop. I slam the door and walk past the café, still full of German soldiers enjoying the autumn sun.

I stop by the bulletin board and spit on a poster announcing yet another food ration cut. My husband isn't in Russia. No one would take him to Russia without notifying me.

"Gabriele, this is for you," I serve him a glass of milk that I had managed to put my hands on the other day.

"Gabriele Di Maggio, Fourth Rifle Regiment, Forward Ranger, Third Motorcycle Platoon." He sips the milk and some of it spills through his bushy beard, dripping down his chin. He remains seated, leaning on the motorcycle. The torn tire was tossed aside, and he'd replaced it with the new one.

"Gabriele, thank you. Can you ride a motorcycle?" I lean next to him, try to approach and hug him, but I can't.

"No, it's too dangerous." He eats the slice of bread I had handed him with the milk.

"Gabriele, teach me to ride a motorcycle."

"It's dangerous. Don't do it. They're going to shoot us." His dark eyes stare at me; and I notice tears welling up in his eyes.

"I'll take care of you, Gabriele. I promise I'll take care of you." I put my hand on his arm, fighting a rising sense of nausea.

"It's dangerous."

"I'll get you some more milk and bread." I continue to caress his arm, and he nods.

"Squeeze the pedal and grab the handles." He stands next to me in the alley. "Gently, twist the throttle," he points, swaying back and forth and looking to the sides with concern. "They'll shoot me."

Two people and their donkey pass by and look at us, but I ignore them. I need to learn how to ride my motorcycle. I need to convince Gabriele to ride the bike with me.

"Please, Gabriele, I need you to get on the motorcycle," I implore him. "I'll take care of you." The motorcycle starts vibrating under my thighs, and I'm trying to get used to the feeling and noise of the rumbling engine mixed along with the pungent smell of gasoline. It's been so long since I've driven with my lost husband, but I mustn't think about it.

I need Gabriele to guide me, at least at the beginning. Then I'll manage on my own.

"There are Germans in the village. They shot me in the previous war." He continues to sway glancing every which way.

"These are different Germans, good Germans," I assure him, raising my voice over the engine's noise.

"You'll take care of me? Promise?" He slowly approaches the motorcycle and places his hand on the seat behind me.

"I promise. The Germans are our friends. We'll drive outside the village, where there are no Germans."

"It's dangerous. We shouldn't do it," he keeps muttering to himself but finally relents and sits on the motorcycle behind me and holds my back. I smile at him and fight the nausea, the urge to vomit. I need his help.

"Change gears with your foot, and lightly squeeze the throttle," he shouts as we drive down the dirt road in a field outside the village. I'm struggling to keep the motorcycle steady.

"Like that?" I raise my voice over the engine's roar and the whistling wind.

"The birds," he shouts back.

"What?" I look ahead on the road, careful not to overturn.

"The black birds," he starts to scream. "Stop, stop!"

"What's wrong?" I yell back at him and slow down.

"Stop, stop!" He screams and hops off the bike before I even come to a complete stop, knocking us both to the dirt road. I try not to weep in pain when I crash to the ground. I do however notice him fleeing in screams through the plowed field, covering his ears with his hands. I look up and see two large German planes landing in the new airfield they've built outside the village. The bottom of their silver wings are imprinted with black crosses.

"Gabriele, stop," I yell at him and stand up. I start chasing him as I ignore my aching legs. The airplanes fly over my head at a low altitude with such a deafening sound that I'm forced to cover my ears.

"Gabriele!" I yell after they land in the airfield. "Gabriele!" I look around and search for him in the field.

"They want to shoot me. You promised you'd protect me," he whines, lying among the dirt clods, curled up in a fetal position and holding his head between his hands.

"I'm protecting you. I banished them." I slowly lean in and hug him, trying to touch him as little as possible, repeatedly promising him that I'd take care of him. "They're gone, the birds flew away. I'm here," I say to him after a long time. "Let's get back to the motorcycle."

But Gabriele refuses to get back on the motorcycle, and I have to hide it in the bushes and return to the village by foot, reassuring him that the black birds won't hurt him again. I shouldn't have taken him with me.

"Where are you, motorcycle?" I walk through the field in the early evening hours, looking for the bush I hid it in. *Why didn't I mark it better?*

"Where are you, my Emanuele?" I ask the first star twinkling in the sky. Why haven't you written to me? Why didn't you respond to the letter I sent you about our son?

"Where are you, bush?" I shout into the darkness, walking and stumbling through the plowed field. "Why did I lose the motorcycle?"

The sun rises when I finally slowly drive back home, exhausted, and filthy. My hands are covered in cuts and scrapes after having dug through the bushes. Raffaele must be crying at home, starving. I'm done crying.

"Did you come back to protect me?" Gabriele asks when I put the motorcycle in the shed. But I don't answer him. I cover the red dirty motorcycle with the tarp and rush home to feed Raffaele.

"I have a way to get to Rome," I say to the butcher the next day, after having patiently waited for the single customer inside to come out.

"How?" He asks me

"What do you care?"

"I need you to deliver something to Rome," he says after looking at me for a few moments. "I'll pay you. Can I trust you?"

"You've known me since I was a little girl. You know you can trust me." I peer at him. I need the money.

"When you were a little girl, you came bursting in and tried to ruin my shop, screaming at me that I was slaughtering cute bunnies."

"But I didn't tell my father that you hit me. I told him that I fell." I inadvertently touch my thighs, feeling the scar through my dress. That was where he hit me with his belt buckle. I refused to shout and cry. I also refused to tell my parents.

He scrutinizes me, and I stand tall in front of him. Then, he walks over to the door and slams it from the inside. "Wait here, keep the latch locked. If anyone wants to come in, just give a shout," he says and disappears into the backroom.

He comes out a couple of minutes later and tells me to follow him. The table is laden with chunks of smoked ham wrapped in parchment paper.

"Take the big package to this address," he places a handwritten note in my palm as he pushes the meat into the burlap sack. "They pay a lot for smoked ham on the black market in Rome."

"And this one?" I point to the smaller parcel on the wooden table. Is that my payment?

"It's for the guards at the checkpoint on the way to Rome. We don't have any other choice." He smiles at me as he drops it into a different burlap sack. "There are three Italian soldiers standing guard. One of them is a sergeant. Hand him the meat."

"And the money?"

"The man at the address in Rome will pay you." He leads me to the back door of the store, so that the German soldiers at the café won't see me.

"I'll pay you back."

"I know." He smiles at me. "You've always been wild, but never a thief."

"Thanks." I load the heavy burlap sacks on my shoulders and quickly walk away. I'll get to Rome and find out what happened to my Emanuele.

"Don't do it. It's dangerous." Gabriele is sitting in the corner of the shed, covered in his old, torn military coat.

"I must," I reply and uncover the motorcycle. I don't have to listen to him, he's a crazy who mostly talks to himself.

"You mustn't go," he closes his eyes and covers his head with his hands. "You mustn't go. You must hide."

"I'm not going to war," I reply while looking for some wire to tie the burlap sack on the sides of the motorcycle. "I'm going to Rome. It isn't dangerous there."

"Gabriele is afraid. They're walking around in the village. I'll come with you." He stands on all fours, and gropes around, finally handing me an iron wire he had found.

"Gabriele, I'm sorry," I try to think what I can say not to offend him.

"You don't have to be sorry. I'm strong. I'll take care of you like you took care of me when the black birds came from the sky." He helps me tie the burlap sack. He forcefully pulls and tightens the iron wire.

"Gabriele, you can't come with me. I'm sorry."

"But why? Gabriele is strong." He turns his back to me. "Why can't Gabriele protect you?" He starts shaking, and I think he might be crying. He can't come with me. He's crazy.

"Because Gabriele has to guard the shed for when the black birds return." I place my hand on his big shoulder, disgusted by the touch of his dirty coat.

"But Gabriele needs to guard you," he continues to whine, shivering in his old military coat. Then drops to his knees again, and crawls to the corner. "Gabriele must be brave, Gabriele must be brave," he whispers over and over to a piece of firewood he'd grabbed from the small pile at the side of the shed. He cradles it like a baby.

"Can you stay in the shed and protect me from afar?" I

approach and caress his hand, trying to soothe him, feeling the shaggy coat and his heavy breaths. When I return from Rome, I'll get him a tub of water and some soap.

"I'll protect you from the shed. I'll look through the cracks," he wipes his tears.

"Thanks, Gabriele. I'll be back soon." I get on the motorcycle and hold the throttle like he had taught me. With a kick, I hear the engine start growling deeply, and the motorcycle begins quivering between my thighs. I gently squeeze the throttle and slowly start driving forward. I can feel the bumps of the cobblestones under the bike, but after a few yards, my foot slips, and the engine stops.

"May I help you?" I hear Gabriele's voice from the shed.

"No thanks, I'll be fine." I stabilize the motorcycle and hit the pedal again, restarting it. I have to succeed without him. He can't help me.

"Good luck," I still hear him over the engine's rumble as I slowly drive away.

I managed to shake him off. Now I have to handle the military checkpoint on the way to Rome. I've got the ham ready for those three soldiers.

When I see the guard's post in the distance, I pull over on the side of the road and look at them, letting myself rest a little. I let go of the bike's throttle, and open my husband's leather jacket, which had protected me against the wind. This is the first I've worn his leather jacket, even though it's been so long since he left me. I press the jacket's lining against my nose, trying to smell his body odor mixed with the smell of the leather. I'm ready.

The ham for the soldiers is placed in the burlap sack tied to the right side of the motorcycle. My monthly cigarette ration is safely stashed inside my pocket. I'll try to offer them my ration and keep the ham for myself.

I touch the inner pocket where I've hidden several bills, just in case the cigarettes won't be enough. I don't eat much anyway, and I can manage without the money. The important thing is that I make it to Rome.

I need to smile politely, explain to the soldiers that I need to continue to Rome, look for the sergeant who commands the checkpoint and tell him I have something important to pass along. When he'll ask if I have documents, I'll hand him the small box with the cigarettes. I won't mind them searching the motorcycle, I've got nothing to hide. I'll just hand him the sack on the right. However, I must deliver the sack on the left. I repeat in my head the sequence of actions that I need to carry out, and my palms start to sweat. They've been sweating ever since I've left the village.

I squeeze the throttle, and slowly drive up the road towards the checkpoint. The checkpoint is a small, white, wooden shack. There's a barbed wire fence on both sides, a grayish military jeep parked on the side of the road, a white and red wooden pole lying across the road. All three soldiers stand tall and examine me.

"Stop." The soldier motions to me as he calmly approaches. His weapon is strapped to his shoulder.

"I'm on my way to Rome." I smile at him politely.

"Do you have papers?" He asks, his looks at my legs, spread apart on the red motorcycle. What will I do if he tries to confiscate my motorcycle? I had promised my Emanuele that his bike would wait for him when he returned.

"Yes, I have." I smile at him and reach for the leather jacket's pocket, as I look sideways and try to locate the sergeant in charge. Who is the sergeant?

"What does she want?" I hear someone asking in German, and notice a German officer leaning against the jeep, holding a walkie-talkie. My hand stops inside the pocket.

What should I do?

"Yes?" The soldier looks at me and places his hand on his rifle's stock. Does he think there's a gun in my jacket?

"What does she want?" The officer asks again, hangs up the walkie-talkie, and starts walking towards us. I can't offer him the cigarettes. I have to do something.

"I made a mistake," I whisper to the soldier.

He glances at me, still holding his rifle's stock.

"Head south," he raises his voice and points. "Look for a dirt road," he whispers to me. "She took a wrong turn," he shouts back to the officer.

"Thank you," I whisper and turn the motorcycle around, quickly driving away on my rattling bike.

Breathe, breathe, breathe.

I pull over next to a cypress boulevard, get off the bike, kneel and try to vomit, but despite feeling nauseated, I fail. My fingers dig into the soft ground. I should have taken some water with me.

A few minutes later, I get up, wipe the sweat off my forehead, put the jacket back on, and sit on the motorcycle. I start looking for the dirt road. I won't give up.

The city has hardly changed since the last time I was there. The only difference I notice are slightly more military trucks and fewer civilian cars on the roads. And of course, there's no husband requesting to take my picture standing next to his red motorcycle. I pull over in that square, among the military trucks and look at the German soldiers taking pictures of their sweethearts. I need to deliver the package and find out what happened to my husband.

"Take a left on the Republic Square, and then right on Via Agostino, next to the fancy shoe store," a young woman gives me directions. I avoid the traffic police officers positioned in the squares; their white-gloved hands gesture here and there, directing what little traffic on the road. I also keep away from the men walking down the street. I'm afraid they'll try to grab the burlap sacks and run away.

"It's on Via St. Ignazio, not far from here," an elderly woman points to one of the alleys. I thank her and drive on, stopping next to a shop with a small sign of a smiling pig's head. It appears to be closed. I've arrived at my destination.

I slowly get off the motorcycle, check the empty alley and check again the address to the crumpled note. This is the place.

I nick my finger on the iron wire when I try to untie the sacks. I can't bandage the wound, so I just suck the blood, and wait a couple of minutes for the bleeding to stop. I have to go in. I use the doorknocker several times, it thuds loudly on the iron door until I hear a latch open.

"What do you want?" A big man in a bloodstained apron scrutinizes me through the door he'd cracked open.

"I have something for you."

"I don't need anything."

"I was told to give it to you." I show him the sack.

"I don't know you. Get out of here." He opens the door a little and looks at the alley, making sure that it's empty.

"I was told to give it to you," I insist. I need the money for the transfer.

"Well, you did, thanks." He grabs the sack and pulls, trying to tear it from my arms, but I manage to hold the sack and enter the dark shop with him. There's a large wooden table at the center of the dim room, it's covered in chunks of meat.

"I need the payment." I hold the sack tightly, glad that I've left the smaller sack outside.

"I can't pay you right now. Get out of here, tell him I'll give him the money next time," he replies, saliva droplets splatter from his mouth.

"I'm not leaving without the money."

Breathe, breathe. I mustn't appear weak. He mustn't think that I'm afraid of him.

"No money." He pulls hard on the sack and yanks it from my hands. I'm forced to let go so he doesn't break my fingers.

"I need the money," I say quietly, reaching into my boot and pulling out the knife I hid before the trip. "I need the money now." I approach him slowly. I clench the knife; my fingers turn white. I hope he doesn't notice my hands are trembling and the sweat on my forehead.

"I'm a butcher." He starts laughing out loud, his filthy white apron shaking with his every movement as he takes a few steps back. "I'm not afraid of knives and blood," he whispers as he grabs a huge butcher's knife from one of the shelves, brandishing it.

"Don't you dare. They'll look for me," I whisper, even though I know I should turn around and leave. I still have a small sack of ham. I've lost this battle. "My money," I whisper. I won't turn around and run away.

He looks at me for a few seconds and draws a little closer,

but I don't back down. Finally, he pulls a couple of bills out of his apron, and throws them at me, "Count them."

"Check the meat," I keep pointing my knife at him, refusing to touch the money.

He tears the burlap sack and examines the ham with his dirty hands. "It's fine. Count the money." He smiles at me for the first time. I still hold the knife as I count, my fingers aching.

"It's okay. It's enough," I pick up the bills and start walking slowly back towards the door.

"You're brave. That's good. We need courage to fight them."

"What do you mean by 'them'?"

"It's none of your business. You got your money."

"Who's them?" I stay put. I feel the cold metal door on my back.

"Those who sent our army to Stalingrad."

"What do you know about Stalingrad?"

"I don't know anything. Go away before I change my mind." He stops smiling and picks up the butcher's knife he had previously placed on the table between the pieces of ham.

I leave the store and approach the motorcycle, noticing the second sack. I was such a fool; I'm lucky no one stole it. I examine its contents and look again at the closed metal door. I don't need meat. Raffaele is too small to eat meat.

"Open up," I shout and hit the iron door again.

"What do you want?" He peers through the crack.

"I've got this." I show him the ham that was intended for the guards at the checkpoint.

"How much do you want for it?"

"I don't want money."

"So, what do you want?" He examines the street.

"I want to know what you know about Stalingrad."

"The ham." He stretches his hand out, and I let him take it. That's my only option.

"Are you one of them? Are you one of the fascists' informants?"

"I'm not their informant." I spit on the sidewalk.

"The BBC reports that the Russians broke through the German lines and surrounded an entire German and Italian troop," he says quickly.

"I already know that. I want money for my meat." I look at him, but I can't reach down to my boot. I shouldn't have put the knife back there.

"Go away. You got the information you asked for."

"But I already knew it. I want money."

"So, you bought it twice. You made a bad deal." He starts laughing again, splattering saliva. "Go to the Ministry of Defense. Maybe they'll tell you everything's okay in Stalingrad." He slams the iron door in my face with a bang.

"Your name, please?" The clerk at the Ministry of Defense asks. He's sitting behind a mahogany desk laden with papers.

"Francesca Morelli," I reply. I've been walking for hours, from one room and floor to the next, each full of men in respectable suits and secretaries wearing skirt suits and high heels, searching for anyone who'll agree to hear me out. Finally, I was referred to this clerk.

"And what seem to be the issue" He looks at my ID, carefully examining the cardboard and my photo, marked with stamps.

"I want to know what happened to my husband." Since noon, I've been addressing clerk after clerk, explaining the purpose of my arrival. Each has referred me to a different department.

"Why would you think something happened to your husband?" He gives me back my ID card and looks at one of the papers on his desk.

"Because it's been months since I've received a letter from him," I put the ID card in my purse. I have to be nice and polite.

"Mrs. Morelli, this is the Ministry of Defense of the Italian Empire. It isn't our duty to try to understand why a man doesn't write to his wife." He lifts his gaze from the paper he was reading and looks at me sternly.

"I just want to know he's okay." I clench my fists but place my hands in my lap.

"Did you receive an official telegram from the government?"

"What telegram?"

"One notifying you if something had happened to him," he doesn't specify what.

"No."

"So, he's fine." He looks back at the paper in his hand. "As you can see, we have a lot of work. We're at war."

"Please, just tell me."

The clerk looks up and examines me, then blurts, "we also have to be careful not to provide information regarding our military units to the enemy. Mrs. Morelli. I think you need to go."

"I have to know." I place the cigarette box and the brown paper envelope full of bills on top of his documents. "I'm not the enemy. I'm his wife."

"What unit did you say he was in?"

"The Second Corps." I'll manage next month without that money.

He thinks for a moment and says nothing but finally takes the box and the envelope, tucks them in his jacket pocket, and stands up. I follow him with my gaze as he walks to the back of the great hall, disappearing between the rows of shelves. As I wait for him seated in front of his desk, I watch the women sitting next to the hall wall. They have a stack of cardboard cards and are typing quickly on the teleprinter devices in front of them, ignoring all the noise around them. Are these the women who send the horrible fateful telegrams?

"Mrs. Morelli," he sits down a couple of minutes later. "Your husband's unit has been sent to Stalingrad, but I can assure you he's fine," he smiles at me. "If you haven't received any other news, your husband is healthy and bravely fighting the enemy. You mustn't listen to cowards or spread their rumors." He leans forward and says seriously. "Have a safe journey back home, Mrs. Morelli." He stands up and reached his hand out.

"Thank you." I stand up and leave the building. I didn't shake his hand.

City Covered in Snow
November 2021, Kyiv, Ukraine

Anna

The snow keeps falling as I emerge from the subway, carefully walking down the white-streaked street so as not to slip on the ice. I head toward grandma's apartment block building. The cold wind freezes my face as I hold the groceries that I had bought for her. It's hard for her to leave her apartment in this weather.

At the entrance to one of the buildings, I pass a man clearing the path with a shovel. I'll stay with her for a short while before I return to the university. I have a lot of studying to do.

"You shouldn't have brought me so many things," she grumbles as I place the bags in the kitchen. "Give me your coat. I'll hang it."

"It's okay, grandma. I'm fine." I remove my coat, scarf, woolen hat, and gloves, putting them at the entrance. I can already hear her from the kitchen putting the kettle on the gas and opening the cupboard to take out the glasses.

"Shall I help you light the gas?" I rub my frozen hands together. The gas oven in the guest room isn't on, and the room is cold. "Are you stockpiling food? They say the Russians will try to invade us."

"No need, Anuchka. I've survived the Germans and Hitler. I'll survive Putin too." She walks around the house in her woolen sweater, but I bend down and turn on the heater. She shouldn't suffer from the cold, certainly not at her age.

"Grandma, I'm sorry," I say as she finally walks into the guest room, placing the teacups on the table.

"What for, Anuchka?"

"I took the old photo from the wooden music box," I fish the picture out of my pocket, and place it on the small table. "I shouldn't have done that. I'm sorry." I hold the glass, warming my frozen fingers. Soon the room will warm up.

"It's okay, Anuchka," she grabs the photo shakily and looks at it. "It's just an old picture from that war. It isn't really important."

"Who is this woman?"

"I don't know. I found the picture in the winter of 1942, in Stalingrad."

"And you just found it and kept it? As a reminder? As a souvenir?" I look into her eyes, looking for a hint.

"I think I took it from a soldier who was there. I don't remember anymore. It's been so many years."

"He was one of them? One of the German or Italian soldiers?"

"It's been so long, Anuchka. The whole city was ruined. Back then, I wasn't working at the tractor factory anymore. They were the enemy, and they tried to capture the ruins of the factory and to reach the river." She noisily sips the tea, her hands tremble.

"Did you fight them, grandma?"

"We had no choice." She puts the teacup down and stops talking for a moment as if trying to remember. "The Volga River was behind us," she pauses again. "The river and the communist officers. They were waiting to see who would back off, machineguns in hand, and in front of us were the Germans and Italians." She brings the glass to her lips. "We had to choose between dying in battle or dying while trying to fall back," she says slowly, sipping her tea. "So, we fought. We crawled like rats in caves through the ruined city. None of the beautiful parks or buildings had survived, there was only snow and ruins. But they died too when winter came. They just froze." She slowly gets up and walks to the display case, takes the key, and opens it.

"Was he dead?"

"Who?" She opens the mahogany music box, and I hear the music as the little dancer spins.

"The soldier, the one you took that photo from."

"Anuchka, even those who lived died a little in that winter in Stalingrad. Both us and them. It was so cold." She shuts the wooden box, and the music stops.

"And what about him? What happened to him? Why won't you tell me?" I watch her as she locks the display case and sits back on the couch next to me.

"Because I'm too old, Anuchka. And I don't want to remember what happened during those days." She smiles at me.

On the way home, I rub my frozen hands together. I can't stop thinking about the woman standing by the motorcycle, wondering if she was looking for the soldier who carried her picture in his pocket in the winter of 1942.

After the Battle was Over
Italy, February 1943

Francesca

"Saint Mary, please help me find my husband." In the dark church, I kneel, cross my arms, and pray silently. She is sure to listen to my words. Only a few candles illuminate the dark church hall, but I know she is watching over me with her kind eyes.

"Saint Mary, please protect my Emanuele in the harsh Russian winter. Please keep him alive in the freezing snow of Stalingrad. Wherever he is, please let him get through the winter alive, that's all I ask of you." I continue whispering as I open my eyes and look at her statue standing above me. She is the mother of all women. She must understand what I am going through. I hear someone rustling through the aisles and notice Cecilia approaching my row of pews. She is still standing at some distance from me when I see her cross herself, kneel down and begin to pray.

"Saint Mary," I look back at the holy virgin, "Please make sure I don't have to wear a black dress like her. I know he's alive. I'm sure he's alive." Since Cecilia started sitting in the café with the German soldiers, we hardly talk anymore. Nobody in the village talks to her, but she doesn't seem to care. She usually sits with them laughing and smoking cigarettes, while they gather around buying her wine and cakes.

"Saint Mary, please help her too." I close my eyes and cross my palms until my fingers turn white. "Please," I get up, walk over to Cecilia, bend down next to her, and continue to pray. I look at her under the candlelight, but she does not respond and continues to pray with her eyes closed.

"Please don't go to them again," I whisper.

"You're interrupting me." She looks up at me for a moment before closing her eyes again.

"You're one of us. You're nothing like them," I keep whispering.

"I'm a widow. I no longer belong to anyone."

"But you're one of us, you're from this village."

"No one in this village talks to me anymore," she said quietly.

"Don't go to them."

She stops praying and looks at me. "It was like this before. Even before I started socializing with them, the people in the village distanced themselves from me. They felt sorry for me and acted as though I was a pariah, gossiping behind my back." She crosses her hands again and looks back at Saint Mary, moving her lips without sounding the words. After a moment she says, "It will happen to you too when you become a widow, you know that."

"Shhhhhh..." Someone behind us whispers, trying to silence us.

"That's not true," I answer, moving a little closer to her.

"You know it's true." She doesn't even look at me but keeps her eyes on the statue. "I'm sure you already prepared the black dress, waiting for the telegram to arrive. They're probably talking behind your back too, waiting for the moment they can pity you."

"They love you. Nothing's changed since we were kids," I whisper to her, but deep inside I know she's right.

"They're afraid of me. I scare all the women here in the

village. They're afraid that my husband's death will infect them. They're afraid of the black dress. At least the Germans are not afraid of me."

"But the Germans are our enemies."

"No, you're wrong. The English and the Russians are our enemies. The Germans are our allies. An English soldier killed my husband, not the polite German officer inviting me for coffee, listening to my stories." She pauses for a moment and then continues. "You're wrong to want to fight the fascists and spread your propaganda against them. You're mistaken for thinking you're smarter than they are." She looks at me, and in the dim light, I can see the tears streaming down her cheeks.

"I'm not wrong. They're responsible for this war and for your husband's death." I regret my words as soon as utter them. I shouldn't have said that.

"You're a proud woman who can't see anything but her pride. You're blind to reality, and I shouldn't have listened to you. Not then, and not now."

"Shhhhhh..." The woman behind us whispers again, but I ignore her. Saint Mary will forgive me.

"You're my friend," I whisper to Cecilia.

"Friends listen to each other."

"I apologize. I'm listening to you now." I close my eyes and cross my palms, but then look at her again.

"I'm a widow." She turns to the altar and pretends to pray. "So, at least I can be a widow who enjoys life a little."

"There are other ways to enjoy life," I whisper to her. "Not just socializing with the Germans and their fascist friends."

"They treat me well; they give me food and listen to me, and when I laugh, they laugh with me. I don't have to stay home and cry like everyone here in the village expects me to."

"But you had a husband you loved."

"Yes, I had a husband who was killed by an English soldier. And now I don't have a husband to love, and neither do you," she continues quietly talking. "Saint Mary has already forgiven me," she pauses for a moment and looks at me. "By the way, there are also a lot of German transport pilots among them from the nearby airfield. They fought in Russia before they arrived here. Maybe they know something that you don't. You should join me one evening." She looks up at the saint, crosses herself, and rises to her feet. I follow her with my gaze as she walks out of the church, leaving me kneeling in front of the statue.

"Francesca, where are you going out dressed like that?"

"Mama, it's none of your business." I stand in front of the open wooden closet door and examine myself in the mirror. I've already changed three dresses, throwing the ones I don't like on the bed. This is the same bed where I made love to Emanuele the night before he was taken from me. It's getting late and I have to decide.

"What would father say if he was here?" She's standing at the door watching me, holding the sleeping Raffaele in her arms.

"Papa would understand, and papa is no longer with us," I answer her, regretting it instantly. I should really think more before I speak.

"Papa wouldn't approve of you talking to me like that."

"I'm sorry." I approach her and give her a hug; I then gently kiss Raffaele on his head and return to the mirror. My fingers quickly unbutton the dress, and I throw it on the bed along with the others, now dressed only in a simple camisole.

"Are you going out to meet them?" She asks, but I don't answer her. I look at myself in the mirror and pinch my waist. I wish I had a curvier body. The last few months have been rough, and food was hard to come by. I notice that my breasts got a little smaller, especially after I stopped nursing Raffaele. The camisole's smooth fabric feels loose against my body.

"Father would not agree to this," she continues.

"Papa tried to fight them and failed." I wipe a tear off my face and tighten the camisole's shoulder strap. "We're on our own now." I finally choose a light cream-colored dress that I tried out earlier but tossed aside on the bed in dissatisfaction.

"Did that friend of yours influence you? I saw who she goes out with," Mama is still standing at the door, but I don't answer her. I examine myself in the mirror. I've been calling this dress the Roma dress since that day. I want to take it off and throw it on the bed again, but this is the best I have.

"You have a child, and you're married. Married women don't do such things."

"Mama, that's enough. I know what I'm doing," I say as I put on the only lipstick I have, pinching my cheeks to give them some redness. "Would you look after Raffaele for me until I return?"

"I don't want you to do that."

"Could you give me some privacy?" I say, and she finally leaves the room, closing the door behind her. I have to finish getting ready, and the dress doesn't sit well on me.

After putting myself together as best as possible, I take one last look in the mirror before heading out.

"Ciao mama. I love you. Please don't judge me." I give her a kiss. As I leave, I can see her standing in the kitchen making tea from plants she collected in the fields, while Raffaele sleeps in his crib next to her.

"I won't judge you, but she will." She doesn't kiss me back but instead crosses herself while looking at me with her black eyes.

"Yes, only Saint Mary can judge me," I answer her, hoping the saint would understand.

"And your husband, your husband fighting in Russia, the one you forgot about."

"Yes, my husband will also judge me, but he will also need to understand" I walk away and exit the house, fighting the urge to slam the wooden door behind me. I don't want Raffaele to wake up.

The street is wet from the rain that fell earlier this evening, and I can hear my shoes hitting the smooth pavement. A gust of cold wind makes me shiver and I hug myself. I didn't take my coat with me. It's too simple for them. It's better that I will be a little cold.

While passing the deserted village square, I stop by the closed cinema and look at the huge canvas poster glorifying the victory in Russia, managing to read the bright letters in the dark.

"Forgive me, Saint Mary for what I'm going to do." I cross myself in front of the poster and then arrange myself.

"Forgive me, my beloved Emanuele, but I know you will understand," I whisper for the last time as I adjust my dress and pinch my face to make my cheeks look red and tempting before entering the café.

The music's noise and the stench of cigarette smoke hits me as I open the café door, rushing to close it behind me. I don't want anyone to notice that I went inside. I lean on the door, making sure it's closed, and look around. The small cafe is full of German soldiers and officers who sit around tables or stand in the corner with their drinks. Some are singing a German song that I don't recognize.

"Lily Marlene," they occasionally repeat a woman's name as they sing about a girl standing under a street lantern, waiting for her soldier to return from the battlefield. "Lily Marlene." They raise their glasses whenever they mention her name and take a sip. I need to get out of here. I can't do this. There are so many of them here. How will I manage to find the one I need?

I notice Cecilia sitting at one of the tables in the corner of the room in a cloud of cigarette smoke. Next to her is a German officer; their table is full of empty wine glasses. I smile at her, but her attention is on her companion, who hands her a box of cigarettes. She pulls one out and lights it with the help of the officer.

"May I invite the lady for a drink?" A tall, fair-haired officer asks me.

I examine the officer's hat and the iron cross around his neck, scanning his uniform for the right insignia. "No thank you." I smile at him politely. I have to find someone else.

Two officers in red paratrooper shoes smile at me from their table and raise their glasses. I ignore them and walk further inside the cafe, pulling out a cigarette and tucking it between my lips. I find myself next to a brown-haired officer in a dark blue uniform.

"Here you go, Mrs." He pulls out a metal lighter from his pocket, and I approach his outstretched hand, inhale the smoke, and smile at him with gratitude. His chest boats an aviator badge. "Can I invite you for a drink?"

"How do you like Italy so far?" I smile at him. "More pleasant than the freezing Russia?"

"Fortunately, I wasn't in Russia. Only few lucky ones got out of there alive," he laughs. "I fought in the desert of North Africa." He sips from his wine glass. "Much more peaceful, with the exception of the English vipers."

"You're lucky. I heard the winter in Russia is rough." I continue to smoke next to him. He won't do.

"He was in Russia." He waves to another a pilot and the officer waves back and invites us to join. "Would you like to hear stories about the snow and the sewer rats of Stalingrad?" The pilot escorts me towards the table and introduces us, placing his hand on my hip.

"We had to light bonfires under the planes' engines so they wouldn't freeze, otherwise we wouldn't be able to start them in the morning." He empties his wine glass. "And the Russians didn't fight us at all. They just let our soldiers freeze to death." He fills his glass again. "But to the outside world they announced that we beat them." He continues to sip his wine as I ask him questions. This goes on for a while. His uniform is full of medals and decorations, and the Black Iron Cross decorates his neck. The other pilot who introduced us is long gone, probably joining his friends singing about Lily Marlene.

"What is it like, landing in the snow?" I ask him, and he explains in great detail while I pretend to be interested. My fingers occasionally touch his arm that rests on the table, and I try to forget what Emanuele's warm hand felt like.

"The Russians hated us, the transport pilots, because we kept the besieged soldiers alive," he strokes my hand for a moment.

"And how did you get out of there? You're a hero." I sip some wine and look at him, trying to catch his gaze.

"It took a lot of courage to fly to Stalingrad's front every day and try to evacuate our soldiers so that they wouldn't be captured." He smiles at me. "You're probably right. I'm a hero."

"I appreciate heroism. Your stories are fascinating." I hand him my glass to be refilled.

"And why is a beautiful woman like you interested in the stories of pilots?"

"I'm not interested in the stories per se. I'm interested in the heroes who are our allies."

"Aren't my stories boring you?"

"Your stories fascinate me. I still have a lot of questions." I touch his palm for a moment, feeling his soft fingers.

"Would you like us to go to a more private place? It's hard to have a conversation with all this singing around us."

"I have a nice place we can go to," I say to him and laugh, fighting my nausea but touching his arm again as if by mistake.

"Would you like to show me this place?" He laughs and pulls out a stack of bills, leaving them on the table without bothering to count them.

"Follow me." I take his officer's hat, place it on my head, and take his hand, leading him towards the exit. I take a bottle from one of the tables in my free hand.

"Good night." It seems to me that we are accompanied by greetings and laughter from the surrounding tables, but I ignore them. I need to get outside to the fresh air. I hope I didn't have too much drink.

"Come with me, my Luftwaffe hero." I walk through the quiet alley, our hands clasped together, as I try to breathe the cold night air. He tries to stop and kiss me a few times, nearing his wine-stained lips to mine, but I turn my head away and just let him kiss my neck, fighting off waves of nausea. I can't stop; not right now.

"Patience, my hero, we'll be there soon. Here, drink this wine," I whisper to him and hand him a sip from the bottle I'm holding, praying that no one will pass us by in the dark.

"Good wine and a curvy Italian woman are all a German pilot needs." He hands me the bottle back and struggles to steady himself, hugging me again.

"Wait here for a moment. I'll be right back." I take a deep breath as we approach my house, and I feel his hands trying to touch my breasts. I move away from him, going up the stone steps to the house.

"Shall I come? Frau Italiana?" He asks, swaying slightly in the center of the alley.

"Shhh... Wait quietly. I'll call you in a minute," I open the house door and quickly enter. "Mama..."

"Where were you?" She is standing in the hall. "Have you been drinking?"

"Mama, take Raffaele and go to your room."

"What happened? What are you doing?"

"Never mind mama, just do what I tell you." I rush inside my room, pull the cotton wool out of my bra, and throw it under the bed.

"I hope Saint Mary will help you." She crosses herself and rushes into the back room, closing the door behind her.

"Come... come up..." I whisper to him. He climbs the stairs and enters the house, holding me in his hands. He kisses me on my lips and tries to force his tongue in my mouth. He smells of wine mixed with sweat, I probably do too. "Wait... come with me." I take him to my bedroom, feeling his hand trying to caress me from behind. "One moment..."

"I thought you wanted to ask me more questions." He hugs me from behind, squeezing my breasts hard, and I struggle not to moan from the pain.

"What about the Italian soldiers? Did you try to save them from the besieged front as well?"

"Italian soldiers?" He grins and continues to forcefully touch my breasts. "No one cared about them. They don't know how to fight anyway. They weren't worth saving."

"You're hurting me." I remove his hands but let him come closer and try to kiss me. I have to know. "I thought you were fighting together."

"Fighting together?" He murmurs. "We were instructed not to evacuate them in our planes and let them die in the snow." He starts laughing. "It's nice that you can choose how to die, by freezing or by a soviet bullet.'

"Enough." I try to push him, but he is strong and pins me against the wall.

"Are you out of questions?" He laughs. "Don't you want to ask me if I like Italian women?"

"No. I'm tired, and you're drunk. You need to get back to your base." I try to free myself from his heavy body pinning me down, feeling his hand lifting my dress and caressing my thighs.

"You promised me something." He grabs my panties and

tries to take them down, making me gasp in pain from the fabric stretched across my thighs. "And we both know what I came here for." I hear the fabric of my underwear being torn and feel his tongue trying to enter my mouth. I have to kick him out. He has to go.

"Enough, enough, you're hurting me!" I try to push him off me with all my might.

"You Italians love romance, don't you?" He laughs and grabs the back of my neck, trying to kiss me again. His mouth smells of alcohol, while his lips are pressed against mine. "Is that how you like it?"

"Get out of here!" My nails scratch his neck as I fight the feeling of nausea.

"Do you like it hard?" He grabs my hand and pulls it to his pants, pressing it against the rough, hard fabric. His other hand tries to lift my dress even more as he forcefully grips my thighs. "Italian whore, I didn't come here for nothing."

I groan in pain, trying to pull back my hand, which he holds down to his pants, but he is too strong, and I can't get free. He's going to rape me.

"Let me go..." I try to push him with my hips, but his hand only climbs further, trying to touch me.

"I like your small resistance effort." He says loudly and presses his body against mine. What if mama hears and tries to intervene? I try to block his mouth with my free hand, but he bites my fingers, and I stifle a scream as his hands forcefully squeeze my breasts. I try to scratch his eyes with my free hands, and while he moves away for a second to protect his eyes, I turn my head and push a finger deeply down my throat, making myself vomit in his direction.

"Dirty Italian." He quickly moves away from me, trying to clean his shirt and pants with his hand.

"I'm sorry, I drank too much." I look at him and don't bother to clean myself, feeling the sour taste in my mouth and the tears in my eyes.

"You're all the same, you Italians. Beautiful on the outside and disgusting when you get too close," he says before getting out of my room. I'm left leaning against the wall, breathing slowly and trying to clean my lips with the back of my hand. I can hear his footsteps in the hallway and the sound of the front door slamming shut. Only then do I drop to my knees and start crying, looking at my beloved stained dress.

"Francesca?" Mama calls me from behind the closed door.

"I'm okay, mama, don't come out." I get up quickly and leave the house, remembering at the last moment not to slam the door behind me. I have to support myself when I go down the stone steps to the alley. I need to make sure that he's gone. By the weak light of the streetlamp, I can see his silhouette as he walks away, disappearing towards the square. "Go away," I whisper, trying to remember his name, but it doesn't matter anymore.

I open the shed door, ignoring the sour taste in my mouth, and make my way to the motorcycle, almost stumbling over the fire logs and scratch my legs in the dark.

"Why did you have to go to war?" I kick the motorcycle. "Why didn't you run away from them?" I kick it again and again despite the fact that it hurts. "Nothing matters anymore. You're dead anyway." I grab the motorbike by the handle and drop it to the ground. "How can you be dead?" I keep yelling over and over at the motorcycle.

"You shouldn't do that." I hear a quiet voice coming from the other side of the shed, but I ignore crazy Gabriele and slam the wooden door behind me. I have to go home. I have to do something.

After washing my face with some cold water, I take the dirty dress off my body and throw it on the floor. Then, I roll my torn underwear into a small cloth ball and burn it at the candle flame, ignoring the pungent smell.

"Francesca, is everything alright?" My mother asks again.

"Everything is fine, mama. Go back to sleep," I answer her and rush to the bedroom, take off my torn camisole, grab a wet rag and get down to my knees. I rub the floor clean. I'm naked and my knees hurt from the cold water and the hard stone floor, but I don't stop. I can't stop. After I finish, I throw the dirty rag aside, take out a clean camisole from the closet and put on the black dress that's been waiting for me in the closet for some time now. Maybe Cecilia was right, and it's time for the black dress.

"Cecilia!" I knock on her house door with force. "Cecilia, open the door for me." I knock again. The bitter-sour taste in my throat is still there, despite me rinsing my mouth and eating mint leaves repeatedly. It started raining again and I could feel the raindrops hit the back of my neck and wetting my black dress. I was shivering from the cold night air. I couldn't fall asleep after what happened with the German officer. "Cecilia, it's me." I hit the wooden door with my fist again, still feeling dizzy and nauseous from all the wine I drank. I could still feel the taste of his disgusting tongue. Could it be that she is still spending time with her German?

"What do you want?" The door finally opens, and she looks at me, dressed in her nightgown.

"Please don't go out with him."

"Who are you talking about?"

"Your German officer, the Germans..." I feel my body shivering in the cold.

"What happened?" She looks at me through the crack of her open door. "It didn't work out for you with your German officer? Do you want me to help you find another one?"

"He's not mine, and he's not yours. We need to stick together; we need to help each other."

"Thank you, but he's helping me already. I don't need more help." She's trying to shut the door in my face, but I shove my foot in the crack, trying to think of what to say to her.

"Cecilia, please, we used to be friends."

"Yes, we also used to have husbands once. You know, sometimes war changes things."

"Is that what you really want? To be with one of them?" I still hold my foot in her door.

"Did anyone ask me what I want? Did anyone ask you what you want?"

"But you can't be like that. You can't go out with them." I'm trying to organize my thoughts and words.

"What other choice do I have? Remaining a widow pitied by the entire village?"

"They don't pity you!" I continue to hold the door. My head hurts from the wine.

"Believe me, they do, and they already pity you as well. You're just too proud to admit it." Despite the heavy rain she refuses to let me in.

"What about our people?"

"What people; the glorious fascist empire that sent my husband to North Africa to die in the desert? Or the fascist

Italian generals that sent your husband to die in the snow of Stalingrad?"

"Don't say that. My husband didn't die in the snow. He's alive, and I'll find him. I'll go all the way to Russia to find him if I have to." I yell at her while fighting my urge to vomit.

"Really?" Despite the weak light, I notice her looking at my soaked black dress. "I see you put the black dress on. It suits you. It looks like even you know he's no longer alive."

"I know he might be dead, but I'm not going to give up. I'll find him," I try to find the right words, feeling that I can't explain myself. "Please don't go out with the German officer."

"Look at yourself," she raises her voice. "You used to be proud. You were a respectable Italian woman. Look what's become of you. Now you're a wet rag, just like our country. You should find yourself a polite German officer like I did. And when you do, don't ask him where he got you the fur coat from, as long as it's pleasant and warm." She manages to push my leg away and slams the door, leaving me standing in the dark, cold and wet from the rain.

"Francesca, once again I'm sorry," the older clerk at the post office says to me a few days later. Every day I arrive at the same time, and every day he gives me the same answer. He gets up from behind his desk and walks over to the counter. Besides him is a German soldier who serves the other clients.

"It's okay. I'll come back tomorrow." I smile at him and go out into the square. I no longer ask him to check the mail bags piled up in the corner.

It's been raining for several days now. I left Raffaele with mama and walked through the village, ignoring the people staring at my black dress.

The giant poster glorifying the Russian battles, which hung on the wall of the cinema hall, disappeared, and was replaced by a poster displaying a farmer and a soldier joining hands and welcoming the spring in victory. But spring isn't here yet and it's cold and wet outside. I carefully cross the square trying to stay warm in my old coat.

The sound of a car engine makes me turn around, and I stop to watch a German officer's car rushing through the square, screeching its tires, and filling the air with a pungent smell of gasoline.

People continue on their way ignoring the car that stopped in front of the café, but I keep standing there. I can see the driver jump out of the car and rush to open the back door.

"Mrs." The driver holds the door open as Cecilia gets out of the vehicle, wearing a fur coat and leather gloves.

"Thank you." She smiles at him, and the officer takes her hand. Our eyes meet for a split second as she and the German walk towards the café. She doesn't say anything and turns to face away from me. As she passes me by, I look down and spit on the pavement.

"Halt," the German officer roars at me. He's wearing a black decorated uniform and a hat featuring a skull. "What did you just do?" He keeps yelling at me in German.

"I just felt sick for a moment," I answer him in Italian and look at Cecilia, but she continues to stand there, holding his arm, facing away from me.

"Apologize to the lady," he yells at me in German.

"I apologize," I say to him, examining the brown fur coat she's wearing.

"Keep walking. I don't want to see you here anymore," he orders me.

"I apologize. I once had a friend that looked exactly like her, but I must be mistaken. I really do apologize." I raise my hand holding the Nazi salute and back through the square.

"One day, we'll get our revenge against women like her," a young man whispers to me as he passes me by in the alley. But before I can answer he disappears around the corner.

I stop by a poster reading "The fascist dagger will defeat the American snake standing at the gate of our nation." The women who gather in the square every morning say that the Americans have landed in Sicily.

The Stars & The Stripes
Italy, April 1944, One Year Later

"Mom, look, a truck," Raffaele shouts excitedly, pointing in the direction of a German armored vehicle passing through the village square, shaking the street pavements with a loud noise.

"Come on, honey." I pick him up and take a few steps back.

"And one more," he shouts happily, waving at the soldiers standing in the armored vehicle. They are wearing steel helmets, and their hands are holding machine guns that are pointed at us. I notice their copper bullet belts shining in the morning sun.

"And one more," he shouts, "Bravo."

There are only a few people standing in the square and watching silently as the German vehicles pass by, painted in camouflage colors and filling the morning air with an engine's roar. The black iron cross of the German army is painted on their sides, and I try to count them but lose count at some point. They keep on passing, one after the other at high speed, deafening us with their noise and giving off a deep scent of burnt gasoline, not stopping for a moment.

"Let me down..." Raffaele tries to free himself from my arms and step down onto the pavement, but I hold him tightly and look at the German tank crossing the square. An officer in a black uniform is standing in its turret and talking into a walkie-talkie.

Some children run along the square and try to outrun the passing Garman vehicles, laughing and saluting them with raised arms as if it were some kind of adventure. *What is happening?*

"They say the Americans are advancing from the south towards the village," I hear a woman saying as I get closer to the fountain in the square.

"I don't believe that the Americans will make it here. The Germans will fight. They never give up," another woman answers.

"Shame on you," one of the women shouts and firmly holds the ear of a sobbing child, dragging him from the square and the group of children who are running and waving toward the Germans. But as the Germans came, they disappeared towards the south exit of the village and the road to Naples, leaving behind only tracks in the square's cobblestones, and traces of an engine scent. What is happening in the south? I keep gripping tightly onto Raffaele despite his protests and turn toward the butcher's shop at the side of the square. Maybe he knows what's going on.

The butcher's door is closed, and I knock on it with my fist, trying to look inside through the dirty glass. There is a light in there.

"Mom, why are you banging on the door?"

"It's all right, honey. I'm not hitting it." I finally release him from my arms after looking down the road as we crossed the square, making sure no more German vehicles were coming.

I hear the latch, and a young girl opens the door. Her eyes are red, her hair disheveled.

"Good morning. Where's the butcher?" I ask her.

"He's gone. I apologize. Please come tomorrow." She pushes the door and tries to shut it in my face.

"Is everything alright?" I put my hand on the handle and hold it open tightly.

"They took him last night." She looks at me and wipes her eyes.

"Who took him? They?"

"Yes, the Fascists. They said he was listening to the BBC, and he was arrested for treason and for spreading rumors of defeatism. I'm sorry, come tomorrow," she slams the door, and I can hear the bolt shut from the inside. What's going on? A gunshot sounds in the distance.

"Mom, watch Raffaele. Stay in the house, don't go out." Despite his protests, I hand him to her as soon as I get home, grabbing a basket and most of the money from the jar in the kitchen. I would try and get some groceries in the market if there were any left.

"Did you hear the shots outside?" Mom asks me.

"Watch him. I'll be back soon."

"We saw a lot of trucks, and Mom held me in her arms." I hear Raffaele tell my mom excitedly as I walk out, closing the front door behind me. The streets leading to the square are empty of people now, and I walk quickly, ignoring the shooting in the distance. When I get close to the fountain, I stop to look around.

The square is abandoned. All the shops that were open just a little while ago, are now closed. The cafe's tables are also deserted, and there are no German gray-blue army vehicles parked outside. Even the post office, which is always open, is closed now. Only two young men I don't know are running across the square, and it seems that one of them is holding a rifle in his hand. They stop for a moment, and one of them paints the words 'Revenge on the Germans and the collaborators' on the cinema wall. He moves the paintbrush in quick strokes, ignoring the black paint leaking, before they continue running and disappear in one of the alleys. In the distance, the gunfire sounds grow louder.

"Mom, help me close the blinds," I ask once I return home and shut the door behind me, locking it with the big bolt.

"Francesca, what's going on outside?"

"I don't know. Maybe the Americans are getting closer. Maybe the Germans managed to stop them. I don't know."

"Did you hear something? Does someone know where the Americans are?"

"Mom, the blinds." I go through the house and close the metal shutters one by one, making sure the bolts are locked securely.

"Mom, I want to see more trucks."

"Tomorrow, honey. It's late now, and all the trucks have gone to sleep." I bend down to hug him. A shot sounds from outside, closer this time. "Mom, help me with the bookcase." I start pushing the heavy wooden bookcase standing in the hallway toward the front door.

"Mom, what are those noises?"

"It's nothing, sweety." I hug him. "Come, I'll sit you on the bookcase and you can pretend it's a car driving up to the front door." I hear another shot from outside.

"They must be searching for all those who collaborated with the Nazis," Mom whispers to me after a while. We had been sitting closed in the house for hours, hearing gunshots from time to time.

"Are you sure? The Nazis are still here," I whisper to her.

"If the Americans are close to the village, then they won't be here for much longer," she answers and crosses herself.

"Do you think that's what they do to those who cooperated with them?" I look at her, and she nods. What about Cecilia?

"Mom, I have to go out for a few minutes." I go to the front door and start pushing the bookcase aside.

"Francesca, no, don't go there." She leans on the bookcase and blocks the wooden door. "I know exactly what you intend to do."

"Mom, I have to." I push the bookcase with all my might, ignoring Raffaele, who started crying.

"You don't have to. She made her own choices, and this is her destiny." She crosses herself again. "It is not your destiny."

"Mom, she was my friend. Don't open the door for anyone. I'll be right back." I hug her, and finally, she moves aside and takes Raffaele in her arms, trying to calm him down as I exit to the deserted street and quickly close the door behind me.

As I run down the street, I stop at the entrance to each alley and check that it is empty. The sun has set, and it is almost completely dark out. This makes it easier for me to try to be invisible while running between the buildings' shadows. I need to know if they've caught her. From time to time, I hear shots and loud noises, maybe explosions, but the streets are empty of people, and white clothes hang on clothing lines from some of the houses like surrender flags. Just a little more. I stop to catch my breath. I must get to her house.

As I was peering from a street end, I notice a German armored vehicle stopping, and several soldiers getting off it. I turn around and run into a different alley. I must return home, but I need to know if they did something to her.

"Raise your arms!" I hear shouting in German. Are they calling me?

"Revenge!" Someone else shouts in Italian, and then there is an immediate flurry of gunshots. A few people running in the street suddenly collapse like rag dolls.

Run, run, run, I still manage to notice a Molotov cocktail that is thrown in the air ignite into a ball of fire once it hits the ground. I keep running with all my might, headed for the nearest alley.

Run, run, run, ignore the young man lying in the street in a pool of blood, his arms outstretched to his sides. Ignore the upside down burned German jeep at the end of the alley. Run, run, run.

I only stop as I near Cecilia's house. I gasp, bending down and trying to relax, tasting the sourness in my throat. *Breathe, breathe, breathe, do not think about what you saw, do not think about the young man and the bloodstain. Do not think about the dead German soldier lying in the street.* I must focus only on what I have come for, and then hurry back home to Mom and Raffaele.

"Cecilia," I whisper as I approach her door. The front door is wide open and broken, as if someone had kicked it. "Cecilia." The house's interior is dark, and I enter, step by step, "Cecilia..." I feel my way to the kitchen, find a candle, and light it, slowly going from room to room. "Cecilia..."

The furniture in the guest room is upside down, and the closet in her bedroom is empty of clothes. The kitchen is also emptied of food. "Cecilia!" I call and intend to leave her house. For the last time, I enter her bedroom and cross myself in front of the Virgin Mary picture hanging on the wall. I hope she managed to escape. She used to be my friend.

"*Raus!* Out!" I hear someone shout in German outside, along with the sound of an armored driving crawler belt. I run to the kitchen, but all I find there is an empty glass bottle. "*Raus!*" I hear the shout again, and an immediate series of shots outside follows, along with the screeching of the driving crawler belt and engine sound. Were they aiming at me, or were they shouting at the nearby houses? What should I do? I put the candle out and get down on my knees, groping my way through the darkness inside the house, while also trying to be as quiet as possible.

Only after I'm absolutely sure they've moved on; I get out of the empty closet and start running home.
Run, run, run. I have to go back. What if they try and break into my house? What will happen to Raffaele and Mom? My chest aches as I finally approach the house. I have to be ready. They won't touch my son. I enter the small shed in the dark. I'll be ready.
"It's dangerous. There is shooting outside, Gabriele Di Maggio, Fourth Rifle Regiment, Forward Ranger, Third Motorcycle Platoon," he babbles.
"Gabriele, help me," I shout to him while panting, holding the motorcycle, and turning it on its side.
"It's dangerous. The Germans are coming," he whispers and sticks to me, trying to hug me with his tattered, smelly old military coat.
"Gabriele, help me. Hold the bottle." I open the motorcycle's fuel tank while it is lying on its side and fill the empty bottle with the fuel that spills from it.
"It's a bomb. It's dangerous. They shot at me, but I didn't run away." He comes even closer to me; his shaking hands help me hold the bottle and pour some of the gasoline out.
"Gabriele, I need a piece of cloth," I shout to him even though he is right next to me, ignoring the smell of gasoline that spilled on my hands.
"He gave me a handkerchief, the man who hugged you on the train." Gabriele is laughing nervously, taking out a dirty piece of cloth from his coat pocket and handing it to me.
"Thank you, Gabriele. Stay here, don't go out." I tuck the piece of cloth into the bottle and leave the shed, crouching

next to the stairs leading to the house while holding the Molotov cocktail in my hand. If they come, I'll be ready. They took my father, they took my husband, but they will not touch my son.

"Raus!" I hear shouting at the end of the street and an engine sound. I huddle behind the stairs, my hand tightly holding the bottle full of fuel. I'm not afraid of them.

"Long live Italy!" I hear shouting in Italian and gunshots. What's going on? Are they approaching in my direction, or retreating? I try to stand up a little and peek around the corner, but I see nothing. I only hear the sound of an engine approaching and the shots that won't stop. Where are they?

Then I see it slowly entering the street from one of the alleys and moving toward my house, slowly, like an ancient monster made of steel. I lean down, pressing my back tightly against the wall's stones. I hear the bullets whistle above my head and feel the wall's crumbling plaster falling on my back and head. I must do it; I must stop him from coming.

Now!

My hand trembles as I light a match and bring it closer to the piece of cloth dipped in the bottle.

Now get up and throw it, don't think. Now!

My legs seem to take on a life of their own as I stand up, spread my arm, and throw the bottle as far as I can toward the armored vehicle emerging from around the corner. My eyes follow the small flame as it creates an arc in the air, and then crashes against the side of the tank and turns into a huge fireball that lights the alley in an orange flame.

Run, run far from the house to the shed, and hide. They will come looking for me. What have I done?

My hand slams the thin wooden door behind my back, but I can still hear shouting in German and shots fired in the streets all around.

Hide at the far corner of the shed behind the remaining firewood. Ignore Gabriele, who is trying to hug me, all trembling. Cover your head with your hands and ignore the shouting and shots outside. They didn't notice me.

"*Raus!*" Someone shouts from outside the shed.

"It's dangerous. You mustn't do it," Gabriele whispers to me.

"*Raus!*" They shout again. What have I done? Why did I think I could stop them? I feel Gabriele's trembling body next to me while he puts the hem of his coat on me, trying to cover me up. Now they will kill us both.

"Goodbye, Gabriele," I whisper to him and release his hands holding me. I start getting up towards the door. I will try to run away. I will succeed.

"*Raus!*" The call outside is heard again, followed by several shots.

Don't think, open the door and run to the alley, don't look back. I will succeed. Only a few dozen steps until I cross the street and escape.

I stand and look at the closed shed door, taking a deep breath.

"It's dangerous," Gabriele's hand grips me tightly as he pulls me back toward the pile of wood at the back of the small shed, and I hit them and fall to the floor, groaning in pain. "Gabriele doesn't run away." I hear his voice mixed with the shouting and the sounds of the gunfire outside while he takes the motorcycle lying on its side, sets it up, sits on it, and starts it with his foot.

"Gabriele," I cry as I try to get up, supporting myself and holding the logs, but he starts driving forward and slams into the wooden door, breaking it wide open.

"Gabriele Di Maggio, Fourth Rifle Regiment, Forward

Ranger, Third Motorcycle Platoon is attacking the enemy, Commander!" He roars and bursts out of the shed. But seconds after he disappears through the open wood door, I hear one shot followed by another.

"Gabriele," I whisper and scratch myself, lying down on the cold stone floor. "Gabriele, what have you done? What have I done?"

Several shots are fired into the shed, and I cling to the floor, covering my head and hold back my screams, trying to be invisible.

Lie down where you are and don't move, no matter what happens outside. Close your eyes. They won't go in, don't breathe.

The bullets' whistles hurt my ears, and I breathe heavily, my lips touching the floor stones, tasting the dirt. The most important thing is to be quiet.

"Move on, cover me forward in the street," Someone is shouting outside in German, and more shots are fired. I don't move. I lie still in my place with my eyes closed. I can't bring myself to think about what has happened.

After a long while, when the sound of gunfire recedes, and I can no longer hear German tanks outside, I crawl towards the shed's open door and look out into the street.

The German armored vehicle is still burning at the corner of the alley and lighting up the dark street, and the red motorcycle is lying on its side at the corner. Gabriele is lying on his back by the shed door, the flames from the vehicle seem to be drawing cheerful wings of light and shadow around his body.

"It's my fault. I'll help you," I crawl towards him and whisper, hugging him through his shaggy old military coat, which is painted with a large, dark stain of blood, but he doesn't answer me. He just continues to look at the black sky and smile. "Get up. It's okay. They are gone." I get up on my knees and try to pull the edges of his coat, but he doesn't move and remains lying on the pavement. "Come on, go back to the shed. I'll get you something to eat," I say over and over, caressing his face illuminated by the fire.

I shouldn't have done what I did. I just wanted to love someone and not be a woman in the middle of a war. I'm saying words in my mind, searching for the right ones, but I can't seem to find them.

"It's dangerous. You mustn't lie down like that," I whisper to him as I close his eyes and slowly get up to go back home.

Two days later, the shooting outside finally ceases, and I move the heavy wooden bookcase, open the front door, and finally leave the house.

"Mom, I'll be right back," I say to her before going down the stairs to the alley, making sure she closes the door behind me

A pleasant morning sun colors the quiet street as I slowly walk and look in all directions. Pieces of white cloth or sheets hung in many windows, slowly fluttering in the morning breeze.

The German tank remains standing on the street corner, burnt and black with soot, its machine guns still pointing towards the sky. But the soldiers who were running and shouting in the streets are gone, and someone moved the red motorcycle that was lying in the street and leaned it on the stone steps leading up to my house.

Gabriele also disappeared. Someone took him. Even the bloodstain that covered the pavement where I hugged him that night, vanished, as if it was never there. It must have been washed away by the rain during the night. I stand for a moment in the alley and wonder if all of that had really happened, or maybe I just imagined that entire, horrible evening.

The shed door is cracked open, and I peek in, tightly holding the knife in my hand as I slowly push it open. I flinch when the door creaks, but a few seconds later, I go inside and try adjusting to the dark, carefully examining the shed.

I can still smell a faint scent of gasoline inside, but the shed is empty, and only a few wooden logs stand in the corner. It takes me a while to get the bike inside and lean it back against the wall. I don't have crazy Gabriele to help me anymore. It feels as if I am suffocating inside there without his presence, and I hurry out, walking toward the deserted alley.

Is everyone still hiding in their houses? Did the Germans retreat north? If the Germans escaped, how would I be able to get information about my husband? They are the only ones who know what happened in Stalingrad. Them, and the Russians who fought there. Could I have lost the last opportunity of finding out what happened to my Emanuele? What was I going to do now?

I return to the shed and silently sit on the motorcycle, holding its handles, but then leave them and bend down, hugging the fuel tank and pressing my body to the cold metal. This is the only thing I have left of him, a motorcycle, and memories. I close my eyes and continue hugging and feeling the metal, letting the tears roll down my cheeks and not trying to wipe them away. Outside I hear voices, but I ignore them. They are talking excitedly, telling each other that the Americans have arrived, wondering who burned the German armored vehicle standing at the entrance of the alley.

After a long time, when the street outside becomes silent again, and the people have all left, I get off the motorcycle and walk towards the village square. I will try to get some food. Tomorrow is a new day. I will not give up.

'To Rome' is written in white letters on the turret of a tank carrying the Stars and Stripes flag as it noisily crosses the square and disappears around the curve of the street, bypassing the fountain that once had a statue of a lion at its head, and is now ruined, marble debris scattered around it.

'To Rome' is written on a blue direction arrow sign which a soldier in a khaki uniform hangs on a ruined telephone pole at the edge of the square. Several children stand around and watch him curiously, helping him hold the sign while he pounds the nails with the hammer he is holding in his hand.

"I need to get to Rome again," I whisper to myself while another tank roars and crosses the square, and the soldiers standing in the turret wave goodbye to the children, throwing candy at them.

"The café is closed until further notice," a soldier in a khaki uniform sitting inside the café says to me as I walk inside. He has an officer's ranks, and he speaks Italian with a foreign accent. Khaki-colored wooden crates with 'US

Army' black letters written on them are placed around him.

"They say you can help me," I answer him, even though it's not true. A few village people are standing in the square, trying to process our new conquerors. All the shops are still closed, and they are looking at the destroyed fountain and the tanks loudly passing by on the main street, headed towards Rome and not stopping for a second. Several khaki-colored jeeps are parked next to the café, and their radio transmitters fill the air with whistles and vague noises.

"I only got here this morning, and you've already been referred to me?" The American officer asks me while instructing a soldier who came in from outside to place another box at the corner. A typewriter and a field telephone are already on the table in front of him.

"Yes, I need a transit permit." I take one of the café chairs standing at the corner and place it in front of him, sitting down on it.

"Ma'am..." he says to me as he picks up the field phone from the table.

"Mrs. Morelli."

"Mrs. Morelli, we just got here. It will take us a few days to get organized. Come back in a few more days. By then, maybe I'll be able to understand what you want." He starts talking on the field phone he is holding, explaining how to get to the village square to someone on the other end.

"Tell him to drive straight down the road until he gets to the broken fountain," I say to him.

"Keep driving on the main road until you get to the broken fountain. I settled in the café in the square." He hangs up and looks at me again. "What did you want?"

"I want permission to go north, to cross the checkpoint. You must also have a checkpoint."

"There is no checkpoint, and there is no north. North is the German army."

"I need to find someone. I need to get to Rome and further north."

"There is no Rome, do you understand me?" He replies impatiently and picks up the ringing phone again. "When you arrive at the village, I am in its center, where the headquarters is. Go..."

"I need to get to Rome." I stand and raise my voice, taking the phone from his hand and slamming it into its place. "Perhaps there is someone left in Rome that didn't run away and knows something. The man from the archives, someone, someone there must know. I had a husband, and he disappeared."

The officer looks at me for a moment and picks up the phone again. I shouldn't have done what I just did. They are our conquerors now. I must apologize to him; he can punish me. I remain standing in front of him, breathing heavily, looking at his brown eyes, his clean-shaven face, his ironed uniform. I won't apologize to anyone. I have a husband to find.

"I'll get back to you soon," he says to the man on the other side of the field phone and looks at me again.

"Mrs. Morelli, I apologize, but Rome is still in the hands of the Germans. You will have to wait patiently before you can start searching for whoever you wish to find. I can't help you. No one can."

"I apologize for yelling at you. It's not your fault. You just wanted to free us from the Germans. You wouldn't understand." I turn around and walk out of this place that used to be a café, not wanting him to see my tears.

"Mrs. Morelli," he calls after me. "Are you looking for a job? I need workers."

"I'm not going to work for you." I stop and turn to him, no longer caring if he notices my red eyes.

"We are setting up a military hospital near the village." He writes something on a piece of paper. "Go there, ask for her. She's the nurse in charge." He hands me the piece of paper, still holding the phone. "Tell her I sent you."

"I don't need your favors. I'll manage on my own." I ignore his outstretched hand holding the note, and turn around, returning to the square. I don't need them to take pity on me and offer me a job. I need to find my husband.

***

"Do you have children?" She asks me as she glances at the papers placed in front of her on the large military metal desk. Her nurse's cap is tightly attached to her silver hair.

"I have a two-year-old boy," I answer, wanting to tell her that I also have a husband, but I keep silent. I don't think she is interested in me as a worker at all. She sits in her office on the second floor of the mansion and keeps reading from the papers in front of her. They took the big building south of the village and waved their flag over it, making it a military hospital. The hall on the lower floor is full of wounded people in beds, nurses in white uniforms walking silently among them. The mansion's large front driveway is now decorated with the Red Cross flag that they spread on the ground. On the other side of the driveway, khaki-colored ambulances are parked near to a pile of fuel drums.

"Are you married?" She looks up from the papers in her

hand for a moment, then goes back to reading them.

"Do you need someone to work here or not?"

"You know," she looks up as if noticing me for the first time, "We're not as bad as you might think we are."

"I'm sure of it," I answer her, not wanting to tell her that the Germans also smiled at us at first.

"I see you're wearing a black dress."

"I will be wearing a black dress until I have my husband back," I answer her and angrily turn to leave the room, slamming the door behind me. I start walking down the stairs toward the first floor. It is none of her business. But when I pass the wounded patients' hall and see all the men lying in the white beds, bandaged and groaning, I turn around and go back up the stairs. I need this job, at least for a while.

I bend down by her door and pick up the metal sign **'Head nurse – Blanche,'** which was attached to the door and must have fallen off when I slammed it, trying to put it back in its place.

"I apologize. I really do need this job." I enter her office again and put the small sign with her name on it, on the table. I couldn't get it back up.

"I don't think you are accustomed to apologizing." She looks at me. I notice the tiny wrinkles on the side of her eyes.

"No." If she doesn't take me, I'll find something else to do in order to bring food for Raffaele.

"What did you say your name was?" She examines me again, looking at my black dress.

"Francesca."

"You can start working here tomorrow. The nurses will explain what you have to do." She signs a piece of paper and hands it to me.

"Thank you, Head Nurse Blanche." I turn to leave.

"And Francesca," she says before I close the door behind me.

"Yes, Head Nurse Blanche?" I stop and turn to her.

"In the end, you will find out that we are nicer than the Germans."

"Yes, Head Nurse Blanche." I close the door behind me and stop myself from telling her that when the Germans were there, I had a chance of finding out what happened to my husband, and now that chance was gone forever.

I quickly go down to the first floor and look for one of the nurses. Maybe they are nicer than the Germans.

"What did you say your name was?"

"Francesca."

"I don't understand how they hired you for this job. Can you even understand what I'm saying to you? I don't think you understand English at all," She stands over me and talks while I bend down on my knees, scrubbing the terra cotta floor of the nurses' room with a stiff brush. I keep cleaning the floor and don't answer her. Better she thinks I'm a stupid Italian who doesn't understand English. From the very first day I started working at this hospital, she has been nasty to me. Some of the other nurses here are nice and give me cigarettes now and then, but she never does.

"After you're done here, please go down to the main hall and clean the floor there too," she continues ordering me. I have been working in the large mansion that was converted into a hospital for a month now, cleaning it from morning to night and improving my English. I need to speak good English if I want to be able to find him.

"Audrey," another nurse enters the room. "We need you downstairs in the main hall. More wounded are expected to arrive this evening."

"I'll be there in a moment." Nurse Audrey stands in front of the small mirror in the nurses' room, taking off her white uniform and ignoring my presence as she throws it on her military bed. She walks around the room in her underwear, searching for clean clothes in the small metal locker on the side of her bed, then dresses. "Francesca," she turns to me as she finishes dressing and fixing her hair.

"Yes."

"Please clean my other pair of shoes. It is under my bed."

"Yes," I answer and continue scrubbing the floor, listening to her footsteps grow faint as she walks down the hall.

"There you go," I whisper to myself as I take her white shoes from under her iron bed, place them neatly on the floor and spit on them. "New and clean." I spit on them again and scrub the wet rag over them, rubbing as hard as I can. "Just as you asked." I look at the shiny and scratched shoes with satisfaction, placing them neatly on the side of her bed. She can continue thinking I'm the dumb Italian.

It is evening by the time I finish cleaning and leave the building. I start walking toward the hospital front driveway, to my motorcycle which is parked on the side of the parking lot next to the fuel barrels, but then I stop and look back at the entrance.

Several khaki ambulances are arriving at the entrance, and some soldiers there are running, opening the doors, and placing stretchers with injured soldiers on the ground.

"I need help bringing them in," someone shouts, but no one is coming. A few seconds go by, and I approach them, bend down and hold the handles of one of the stretchers. Another soldier holds it from the other side, and with his signal, we raise it together and begin to carry it inside.

"To the operating room on the left," someone instructs us, and we turn and place the wounded soldier on the operating table. I look at the doctor and the nurses, who are already wearing masks and begin preparing him for surgery.

"There are more outside," someone informs us as we return to the entrance. I ignore the sweat running down my back from the effort as I bend down, hold the next stretcher's handles, look at the wounded soldier, and stop. It's a female soldier.

"Hurry up, she's lost a lot of blood," someone standing next to the ambulance says, and I gasp and get up. I start carrying her inside with the other soldier, looking at her as I walk.

She has wavy brown hair, scattered, and caked with mud, and her handsome face is full of blood stains that have also soiled her khaki uniform.

Carry her, don't stop walking, do not think about her clenched fist resting on the stretcher and her closed eyes. Do not look at the white bandages that wrap her crushed foot. The important thing now is to take her to the operating room. Is she still alive?

"She was a nurse. German planes attacked a military hospital on the front," someone says when we place her on the operating table, but I don't stay there to listen for more.

I leave the room. I don't care anyway. This is their war, not mine. I'm the dumb Italian.

Still, a few minutes later, next to my motorcycle at the end of the parking lot, I bend over and throw up, feeling my sweaty forehead. I will rinse my mouth when I get home.

"Francesca, is everything alright?" Mom asks me later when she enters my bedroom late at night.

"Yes, Mother, everything is fine." I open my eyes for a moment and then close them again, continuing to clasp my hands while leaning in front of the small wood Virgin statue hanging above my bed.

"Holy Mary," I whisper. "Please make this war end quickly and help me find out what happened to my husband. And also take care of the female soldier. Please don't let her die." I cross myself and get up, walk over to the bucket of water in the kitchen to wash my face before bed.

"Francesca," Audrey calls me a few days later.

"Yes." I lower the metal bucket I'm holding and look at her.

"Do you know who hung the small statuette of the Virgin Mary on the wall above the wounded nurse's bed?" She asks me. I pretend not to understand and walk away from her.

"Take it down. This place is a hospital, not a church," she calls from behind my back, but I ignore her and get down on my knees, starting to clean the floor under the female soldier's bed.

Her amputated leg is covered with white bandages, and most of the time, she is either drugged with morphine or moaning in pain, grabbing the sheet with her white fingers as if trying to tear it off.

"It's okay, you'll be fine," I whisper to her in the evening when I take down the Virgin Mary's statuette off the wall so that that nurse doesn't throw it away. Then, I look at the dark and silent wounded hall to see that the shift nurse is far away, and so I cross myself and tuck it under her bed mattress. She needs someone to look after her. I wet her sweaty forehead with a cold cloth, even though my job is to clean and not to help the wounded.

"Thank you, nurse," she sighs and whispers to me, her eyes closed, and I caress the palm of her hand holding the sheet and go back to cleaning, but not before I take the box of cigarettes placed on the metal cabinet on the side of her bed and tuck it in my dress pocket. Every few days, they give her packs of cigarettes, like all the other wounded soldiers here, but she doesn't smoke and doesn't need them anyway. She receives her morphine which helps her to relax.

"You're done for the day. You can go home," one of the nice nurses says to me later, but even though I'm headed for the exit, I stay sitting on the stairs going up to the second floor and listen to them. They quietly talk about the lists of the wounded or gossip about each other, sometimes even mentioning the stupid Italian woman. They have a big brown radio in the shift room which plays soft music from the BBC in London, and sometimes the news. I enjoy listening to it. Later, after resting and wiping off the sweat from the day's work, I cross the dark front driveway of the hospital, hearing my steps on the gravel outside. Sometimes I spot an owl standing on one of the cypress trees. My fingers caress the fuel tank of my motorcycle that has been waiting for me all day before I sit on it and start it with a kick. I drive home carefully in the dark, concentrating on the weak flashlight that lights my way on the ruined road leading to the village.

"How was he today?" I hug Mom when I quietly enter the house, as I approach Raffaele's little bed, lean down, and give him a gentle kiss on his forehead, the kind that will ensure he will have sweet dreams.

"Come, sit. I'll give you something to eat," Mom whispers to me and places a heaping spoonful of risotto on a plate waiting for me on the small table in the kitchen.

"I'm not hungry. I'll eat later." I light a cigarette and go to the bedroom. The old suitcase is waiting for me under my bed, and I get on my knees and take it out, tucking the box of cigarettes I brought today and adding it to the stack that is already there. Then I carefully open the map I once took from Head Nurse Blanche's office and spread it out on the floor, starting to mark lines with a pen.

The BBC reported tonight that the Russians have captured Kyiv and are moving west against the Germans, and I bend down and search for it on the map, trying to read the names of the cities written in English. My fingers mark a new front line that crosses Kyiv with the blue pen. The war will not last much longer.

"Francesca, what are you doing? What have you got under the bed?"

"Nothing, Mother, leave me alone. I'll be right back." I remain on my knees on the floor and look at the map spread out in front of me.

"Why don't you go and ask them?" I hear her.

"Who?"

"His family. They must know something or can at least find out."

"Because they are Fascists," I turn my head and answer her.

"You're proud and stubborn. That's what you are." She leans on the doorframe and watches me.

"The friend I once had said the same thing." I turn my head back and look at the map again. I will not ask for their help. They support the Black Shirts.

"At least she was right about something," Mom says quietly. "Did you hear anything from her?"

"No, Mother," I answer her as I search for Stalingrad on the map. "Maybe they caught her in the end and took revenge. Maybe she ran away to Germany. Maybe I'll never know. There are too many things I don't know in this stupid war."

"At least I know you're a faithful woman. I'm sure of that." I feel her palm stroking my hair. "Come eat. The food is getting cold."

"One moment, Mom." I put the cigarette out and measure the distance from Italy to Stalingrad, placing my palms with my fingers spread on the map, but even my two spread fingers are not enough to cover this distance.

"I'll be waiting for you in the kitchen." She touches my shoulder and walks away while I'm still bent over the map.

"Thanks, Mom," I say and wipe my teary eyes with my hands. I fold the map and stuff it into the old suitcase, close it and shove it back under the bed. Then I cross myself in front of my wall and the faded sign on it, where the statue of the Virgin once hung, and get up and go to the kitchen. Tomorrow I will try to get some gasoline from the pile of fuel barrels placed at the corner of the Hospital's front driveway.

"Let me help you." She hobbled on crutches after me a month later. I walk through the garden behind the hospital among the wounded soldiers and serve them orange juice in enamel cups, and she follows me. "My name is Grace." She stops in front of me and gasps, leaning on her crutches and holding her hand out for a handshake.

"I know your name," I say and keep walking. I do not shake her hand. If she had been a little more sensitive, she would have seen that both my hands are occupied holding the tray of juice cups.

"Please let me help you. I want to get better." She continues to follow me in the garden among the wounded who are sitting on the white chairs enjoying the afternoon sun.

"I'm not going to be your friend." I stand and look at her. She is panting.

"I don't want to be your friend, either. I want to do something."

"There you go, you can distribute your American juice to the wounded. Try drinking real orange juice sometime before you destroy our orange trees with your tanks," I answer as I place the tray full of glasses on one of the tables and walk away.

"Next time, try not to be so friendly to the Germans, so we won't have to come here to rescue your people from them, and lose a leg being attacked by a German plane." I can still hear her.

"Next time, I won't bother to put the statue of the saint

under the mattress you sleep on, asking her to keep you alive," I say to myself and walk away to one of the corners, sitting on the floor and lighting a cigarette. I don't need a new friend that will inevitably leave me one day as well.

"Are you a widow?" She asks me later, when she finds me sitting in the secret corner, hiding. She is standing in front of me, covered in sweat, wearing white hospital pajamas like all the other wounded. "Is that why you always wear a black dress?"

"Why me?" I ask her. Maybe I shouldn't have answered her at all. Perhaps it's better that she thinks I'm the stupid Italian, just like everyone else does.

"Don't you know how to be nice?"

"It's none of your business whether I'm a widow or not." I look up and examine her, her bandaged amputated leg, her white shirt full of sweat stains, and her face looking at me. Her eyes are brown, lighter than mine, and she is staring at me now. "Do you have a cigarette?" I ask her after a while, even though I know she doesn't smoke. But she takes a pack of cigarettes out of her shirt pocket and hands it to me.

"What happened to him?" She places the crutches on the nearest stone wall and hops towards me, carefully sitting down next to me without asking if I'm interested in her company.

"What happened to your leg?"

"Tell me, and I'll tell you."

"I don't know what happened to him." I light the cigarette and exhale the bitter smoke. "He disappeared during the war."

"And they didn't tell you? No one knows?" She continues to question me.

"No, the honorable generals sitting in Rome were too busy polishing their ranks to send telegrams to all the women who were left behind."

"So, you didn't get a telegram?"

"How would I have received a telegram? First, the fascists took over and forced him to enlist, then the Germans occupied us, and now you have occupied us, even though you are trying to be my friend." I look up at the sky. "Now, the road to Rome is blocked by the German army, and there are no more telegrams. Before that, there were only Russians and Germans, and now there is also you. You don't really understand war."

"I understand enough, believe me." She touches the bandage wrapping her amputated leg. "I'm also learning to understand disgusting Italian women."

"The stupid Italian women," I correct her and inhale my cigarette. "That's what they call me."

"If you didn't get any information, then maybe he survived. You can't know for sure."

"He was in Russia, in Stalingrad, in the winter, facing the Russian army. What are the odds that he survived and was captured by them?" I look away from her. I don't want her to see the tear at the corner of my eye. "I'm not that stupid of an Italian."

"You never know." She takes a cigarette out of the box and plays with it between her fingers.

"No, you can never know." I watch her. "What happened to you?"

"A German plane shot at me, one of your friends."

"Yes, one of my friends." I put out the cigarette.

"I wanted to be a nurse who helps the wounded. I still want to be one."

"Who knows, maybe one day it will happen." I look away, knowing it won't.

"You don't believe that is going to happen," she whispers, caressing the bandage on her leg. "They want to send me back home, but I intend to stay here and go back to being a nurse. I will not give up."

"Even if you stay, you still can't be my friend."

"I don't want to be your friend." She supports herself with her hands on the stone wall and rises, bouncing to her crutches on one leg. "And I don't need the Holy Mary that you put under my mattress. I'll do without her." She throws the cigarette box at me and hobbles away, leaning on her crutches. "See you tomorrow at the American synthetic juice distribution to the wounded, and good luck finding your soldier husband alive."

I continue smoking as I watch her waddle away, knowing she is wrong and there is no way he could have possibly survived.

The Ruined City
November 2021, Kyiv, Ukraine

Anna

"Thank you, Mariusha," Natasha smiles at her as she places two slices of cinnamon apple pie in front of us.

"You should eat more. You're both too thin." Grandma says and heads back to the kitchen. I can hear her opening the refrigerator.

"Thank you, grandma, that's enough. We don't need any more," I say to her, hoping she'll hear me. I had asked Natasha earlier if she wanted to come visit grandma with me, and now we're both sitting in her guest room in front of several plates stacked with sweet pastries, and a couple of teacups. "Do you have enough food? Do you need me to get you more?" I raise my voice, hearing her open a jar in the kitchen.

"Don't bother. I have enough," she replies.

"Grandma, they say on the news that the Russians' tanks are advancing to the border. It's not just threats anymore."

"Just eat and be good students," she says from the kitchen. "I've seen enough. I'm not afraid of another war."

"Mariusha," Natasha stands up and cries out, she heads to the glass display case at the corner of the living room. "Is that you in the picture? Is it from before the war?" She looks at grandma's picture in the silver frame; she was younger and her hair a dark shade of black.

"This is me a few years after the war." Grandma comes walking from the kitchen and places another plate of chocolate-covered marzipan on the table. "Taste some of those too."

"Do you have any photographs from the war?" Natasha keeps asking, and Grandma approaches and stands next to her.

"No, honey," Grandma answers. "We didn't have cell phones and cameras like you do today. Back then, very few people had cameras. Only photographers on behalf of the Communist Party were allowed to take photos." She opens the display case's glass door and holds the picture in the silver frame. Her wrinkled fingers brush over the glass, seemingly removing dust, even though it was squeaky clean.

"What did they photograph during wartime?" I approach and stand beside them, take the picture, and look at how beautiful she was.

"Who?" Grandma turns to me.

"The communist photographers, in the war, in Stalingrad."

"They took pictures of the ruined city," she sighs. "Only after the Germans and Italians surrendered, they dared cross the river and take pictures of the ruins. Before that, they left us alone to fight against them through ruins and burrows. They were afraid to cross the river and that the German Stuka diving planes would shoot them." Grandma smiles to herself.

"And what about prisoners? Were there Italian and German prisoners there? Did they take pictures of them?" Natasha asks grandma and reaches for the wooden box inside the display case. "May I?"

"It's just a wooden box." Grandma offers it to her. "There were prisoners of war there. I remember seeing them walking through the snow in long convoys. It was so cold."

"And did you talk to them?" Natasha continues asking.

"We were too weak to speak," Grandma says slowly. "We just looked at them. Some of us took their coats. We were cold too. Some took their food, wanting them to die." I look at her fingers trembling around the wooden box.

"And the picture, the one of that woman standing next to the motorcycle, did you find it in a captured soldier's coat?" I can't help myself. "You told me that you found it on one of their soldiers."

"I don't remember what I've told you. Perhaps he was dead." She looks at me, puts the wooden box into the display case, and locks it. "When you're old as I am, Anuchka, it's hard to tell reality from imagination." She sits back on the sofa. "After the fighting in the city was over, all I wanted was for the war to end so that I could go back home and work on our farm here in Ukraine."

❦

"Did you give her back the picture of the woman?" Natasha asks me as we walk through the snow to the metro station.

"Yes, I gave it back to her on my last visit. I felt bad about it." I pull down my coat's hoodie and feel the cool wind and snow falling on my head as I walk down the street. Was Grandma so cold back then during the war?

"And did she say anything else?"

"You heard her. She told me that day that she took the picture from a German soldier in Stalingrad, and today she said she doesn't remember and that perhaps he was dead after all."

"And do you believe her?"

"I don't know anymore. Maybe he really was a dead soldier." We head down the metro stairs. "Anyway, I gave her back the photo. So, it seems the woman on the motorcycle will stay forever in grandma's little wooden box in the display case."

"Do you think your grandmother would have taken a picture from an unimportant German soldier who died in the snow, and kept it next to the medals she received in the war without any reason?" Natasha speaks as we validate our tickets and head down to the metro platform.

"Maybe she just took a souvenir from the war." I rub my hands together as we wait for the train to arrive.

"It seems to me that she's hiding something," Natasha says. "Even you don't believe it."

"Even if that's true, we have no way of finding out." We walk into the metro that has arrived. "Even if he were alive, we don't even know his name."

"What was the woman in the picture called?"

"Francesca Morelli," I reply and look at the ads on the metro screens, urging citizens to prepare for the approaching Russian threat.

"Perhaps we can find out," Natasha says. "If the woman in the photo was his wife, then at least we have the last name."

"And what if that woman was just his sweetheart?"

"If she was just his girlfriend, then we'll never know what happened," she replies. We stand closer to each other as people start pouring into the metro after their long day at work.

"We could try the university's history department. Maybe someone there will know something." I look at the other people in the car while the metro speeds through the black tunnel.

"In Stalingrad? An Italian soldier?" The head of the history department asks us the next day. "Most Germans who fought there died in the winter of 1942, including the Italians who fought with them. In fact, the Italian soldiers were in a worse condition because they didn't receive a lot of provisions," she continues talking as we both sit across from her in her spacious office. "Why do you want to know?"

"We found an old photo that belonged to someone who might have been there," I tell her.

"In Stalingrad, in the battles of 1942?"

"Yes." We both nod. "We think he was an Italian soldier, and might have survived," Natasha says, even though we're just speculating.

"If he survived, he must have been captured. We have no evidence of people who survived the siege on Stalingrad. Besides, most of those who were captured died within a couple of months. Frankly, considering what they'd done to us, they deserved it," she says dryly. "Do you know what his rank was?"

"No," I reply. "Does it matter?"

"If he was an officer, it could. Officers survived longer in captivity." She fidgeted with her reading glasses placed on her luxurious desk. "That's how things were back then. Officers ate better and didn't work as hard, and those who worked less stayed alive."

"And what if he was a simple soldier?" I ask, but she doesn't reply. She just continues to play with her reading glasses.

"Are there lists of prisoners of war seized in Stalingrad?" Natasha asks.

"Do you know his name?"

"Yes," I reply, even though we may only have the last name.

"I assume that the Red Army archives have included lists of POWs who arrived at Bektovka after Stalingrad. The NKVD liked keeping everything. They must have kept this too."

"Where is Bektovka?" I ask.

"What is the NKVD?" Natasha adds.

"Bektovka is the POW camp south of Stalingrad where they were taken to," she says. "If you'll find his name on the lists, perhaps he survived, but even those who survived the camp were dispersed as forced laborers all over the Soviet Union when the war ended."

"And what is NKVD?" I repeat Natasha's question.

"They were here before the KGB and before we were separated from Russia, who now wants to conquer us again." She smiles faintly. "Try the Red Army archives. Maybe they'll have the lists. It would be best if you submit an official request. The librarians there like official requests. But don't get your hopes up. Chances are he died." She grabbed one of the papers on her desk, signaling that the meeting is over.

"Can you provide us a formal request?" I ask, and she puts the paper down and looks at me. My finals don't start until next week. I have some time, and I can't stop thinking about the woman in the photo, wondering if she was looking for the soldier who carried her picture in his pocket throughout the winter of 1942.

Rome
Italy, August 1944

Francesca

"Francesca, look..." Grace walks towards me, a few months later, limping slowly on her wooden leg and using a walking cane. She's already wearing khaki uniform with the US Medical Corps insignia on her shoulder, although the other nurses still won't let her be one of them. Maybe that's why she keeps visiting me in my own private resting spot that I found in the hospital's garden, behind an old shed.

"What?" I look at the newspaper she is holding in her hand.

"Rome has been liberated," she reads out the English title to me, although I can figure it out from the large, black letters and the image of the soldiers waving the stars and stripes flag at the foot of the Colosseum.

"It's an old newspaper," I tell her, even though I know it's not true. The women drawing water from the destroyed fountain in the village square have been saying for several days, that the Germans have retreated from Rome. I hate that city.

"You know that's not true," she remains standing in front of me while I sit on the ground and look up at her hands that are holding the newspaper.

"What does it matter? First, the Germans were lords of Rome, and now you'll be lords of Rome."

"It matters because you don't have to wait for the war to end. You can go to Rome and find out what happened to your husband." *Why did I tell her about my husband? Why does she care about me at all?*

"It's none of your business what happened to my husband. I don't need your help for anything other than cigarettes. Do you have any?" I hold out my hand.

"What does it matter if I have cigarettes or not, especially since you tend to take them from my locker whenever you want," she raises her voice at me.

"I didn't ask for your help with my husband, and I'll decide whether or not to wait until the war is over," I also raise my voice at her, not interested in telling her why I don't want to go to Rome.

"I'm not going to help you either. You can't be helped," she shouts at me. "You're a stubborn Italian who thinks she knows better than everyone else. No wonder you don't have any friends," she throws the newspaper at my feet, turns, and limps away.

"You don't have any friends either. That's why you came to the stupid Italian woman," I still manage to shout after her, just before she's gone. My hand is searching for the pack of cigarettes in the pocket of my black dress, lighting one with trembling hands, can't stop wiping my tears. I'm afraid of that city.

"I didn't mean it. I'm sorry," she comes and sits next to me after a few minutes. "But I think you should go to Rome."

"I've only had bad luck at that city," I look away, examining the cypress trees around us, and wiping my tears. "And I'm sorry, too."

"I didn't know," she softly says.

"Bad things started long before you arrived."

"So, you might have to wait for the war to end," she takes out a cigarette and lights it for herself.

"Yes, only evil comes out of that city and this war," I look at her hand, holding the cigarette, wondering when she started smoking.

"Don't you have a way to search for information from here, without going there?"

"No," I reply, knowing I'm lying.

"I'm sorry I called you stubborn," she says after a few minutes of us sitting in silence.

"It's okay. My mother also says I'm stubborn and proud," I look at the upright columnar cypress trees around us, moving lightly in the wind.

"Is she right?"

"Let's go. There's something I still want to do," I stand up and give her a hand, helping her up, and we both walk to the hospital's front driveway, to my motorcycle. "I'll give it a shot, even though I am stubborn and proud."

I park the motorcycle at the village square, watching the women gathered near the destroyed fountain, patiently waiting their turn to fill the water in the galvanized steel bucket they're holding in their hands. All the ruins left around after the fights were cleared out. Even the café, which served as a military headquarters in the first days, returned to being just a café. Some older men sit on chairs outside, in the sun, and look at us curiously as I helped Grace off the motorcycle, my hand in hers.

"They're watching us," she whispers.

"You have no leg, I'm a widow in a black dress, and we both ride a motorcycle. Of course they'll look at us," I reply. "Come on," I start walking towards the post office as she follows me.

"Francesca!" The white-haired older man comes out

from behind the counter and hugs me, putting his wrinkled hands on my shoulders. "You haven't been here for such a long time. I've already thought the worst had happened, and you've gotten the message."

"I'm still waiting," I hug him back and ignore the tear running down my cheek.

"I'm sorry," he tells me. "But I still don't have anything for you. You know we can't contact them anymore," he points at the old board with the telegram fees table. Since the Americans arrived, Germany's been marked in a thick red line.

"And what about Rome?" I look at Grace. She stands at the entrance to the small post office, looking around, and I signal her to enter.

"You can try calling Rome on the phone, through the operator. In the last few days, since it was released, you can sometimes get a line."

"Can you please call for me? I have the number," I take a crumpled and stained piece of paper out of my wallet; the note that Emanuele gave me on the day he left for the last time.

"Whose number is it?"

"His family's. They have a phone."

"I'll try," he smiles at me. "How would you like to call, collect?"

"Yes," I awkwardly smile. I have no money left.

He walks to the black phone on the counter, picks up the handset, starts talking to the operator and asks her to transfer him to Rome. The teleprinter marked with the Nazi emblem, which used to be on the back table, is gone, and there's also no polite German soldier to watch over the mail.

"Yes, Roma. Four, four, two, eight," he raises his voice as

he holds the handset. "A collect call from Francesca Morelli. Sì."

I watch him while he waits and at Grace who's standing next to me. I can hear some children running outside and laughing in the square.

"Sì, Sì, I understand," he speaks to the operator and puts the black handset back in its place. "Francesca, I'm sorry," he smiles awkwardly and hands me back the crumpled piece of paper. "But they aren't willing to accept your collect call."

"Never mind. No news can arrive from the Russian front anyway." I turn and walk to the post office exit. "We have to hurry and get back to the hospital, I have a lot of work to do."

"What's the problem?" Grace walks after me in the square, carefully limping on the smooth cobblestones.

"There's no problem. Everything's fine."

"Then why didn't you talk to them?"

"Because they're not home," I stop and turn to her. Why doesn't she walk faster?

"I don't understand," she stops.

"What don't you understand? I have no money," I speak quickly. "I'm a stupid Italian woman who married a charming man with a disgusting family who won't accept a collect call from me. What's not to understand about that?" I raise my voice. "Now, do you understand why I hate that city?" I tear up the note containing his phone number, throw the pieces on the pavement and turn around, continue walking toward my motorcycle. "Come on, let's go back. I have a hospital to clean." I say, but as I get to the bike and turn back, I see that Grace isn't behind me.

She limps back towards the post office, and I let go of the motorcycle and rush after her.

"How much does a phone call to Rome cost?" She asks

the old clerk in English, but he looks at her and doesn't understand.

"She wants to know how much a call to Rome costs," I explain to him in Italian.

"A lot, *Seniora,* fourteen lire per minute," he speaks to her in Italian.

"He says it's a lot," I translate.

"Is this enough?" She takes a stack of American dollar bills from her uniform pocket and places them on the table.

"*Sì.*" he looks at her and takes one bill. "*Sì.*"

"*Sì,*" Grace replies and places the torn pieces of the crumpled paper on the counter. "*Sì.*"

"*Sì,*" he says back, picks up the black handset, and starts talking to the operator again. Then, he hands me the handset, and I bring it to my ear.

"Hello, is it the Morelli residence?" I raise my voice, trying to overcome the noise over the line.

"Who's asking?" Someone on the other end answered.

"Francesca, Emanuele's wife. Have they heard anything from him?"

"Just a minute," she replies and leaves me to wait, and all I can hear are the noises on the line.

"Did they answer?" Grace asks me. Her ear is close to mine, even though she doesn't understand Italian. The old clerk also stands close to us and listens.

"Good afternoon." I hear a woman's voice on the other side of the line.

"Good afternoon, this is Francesca Morelli speaking, Emanuele's wife."

"Hello, how can I help you?"

"I wanted to know if you received any news from him. A letter or a telegram," I feel like I'm slurring my words from excitement.

"Emanuele is at the front, and everything is fine with him," says the woman on the other end of the line, her voice fragmented.

"Is he okay? Did you get a letter from him?" I shout and hold Grace's hand tightly.

"I promise you he's fine," she tells me.

"But I didn't get any letter from him. Did you get a letter from him?" I hold the handset tightly to my ear, trying to listen to the answer, despite the noises on the line.

"If he doesn't send you letters, maybe he has a reason," I can hear her say.

"But I'm his wife," I shout into the receiver, waiting for an answer and feeling Grace's warm fingers holding my hand.

"The line is disconnected, Miss," I hear the operator woman say. "Would you like me to try to connect you again on a new call?"

"No thanks," I put the handset back in its place. "Let's go," I say to Grace. "We're going to Rome."

It takes me a while to find their house in the fancy neighborhood, and we pass by a high, cream-colored wall surrounding it twice, not sure it's the right place. I was here only once before the war.

"I think it's here," I finally shout to Grace, trying to overcome the motorcycle's engine, as I stop by the side of the road and look at the large building with the green shutters behind the high, cream-colored wall.

I park the bike and look at the wide street. There are no donkey or horse-drawn wagons, and it doesn't smell like horse manure. A shiny, black car drives past us quietly, and a man in uniform gets out of the house and hurries to open the main gate, standing upright as the car passes him. I was only here the day he introduced me to his parents. That day, the tears I shed prevented me from seeing the entrance gate Emanuele opened for me, while holding my hand.

"Shall we go in?" Grace asks after she carefully gets off the bike.

"Yes," I wipe the tear from the corner of my eye and look at the big building. The Star-spangled banner hanging by the entrance replaced the Fascist Party's flag that was here when I arrived that last time. "Let's go," I tell her and start walking towards the entrance. "This is the place."

"Wait here, please," asks the maid, who opens the door for us, and we remain standing in the entrance hall, looking at the stairs leading to the second floor. She didn't invite us to sit down.

"Does all of that belong to your husband?" Grace whispers.

"It's his family's," I whisper in reply. The door of the large guest room is partially open, and I can hear voices talking and laughing, perhaps in English.

"I don't think they like you."

"You're right."

"Why don't they like you?" Grace asks me. We've been waiting for a long time.

"Because I'm a simple woman," I reply, looking around at the collection of Chinese porcelain vases that decorate the entrance. "And also, I once yelled at them, sharing my opinion about them and who they were supporting."

"When?"

"At my wedding," I look at the iron-clad knight armor placed at the foot of the stairs leading up to the second floor. Grace says nothing, and we both remain standing in the foyer.

"I'm sorry," the maid tells us after a few minutes, as she leaves the guest room, making sure to close the door behind her. "They can't see you right now, but they want to tell you that you have nothing to worry about."

"Thank you," I tell her and start walking towards the guest room's closed door.

"Francesca," Grace grabs my hand and tries to stop me. "No..."

"I want to talk to them," I release my hand from hers and continue walking.

Are they telling me the truth? Is he fine? Did he stop loving me? Go, open the door, and ask them, no matter what they say, I have to know.

"Please, miss," the maid stands in front of the closed door and blocks it with her body. "Please, I have to keep my job."

"I have to know," I try to move her away from the door while Grace tries to hold my hand and stop me. I have to know.

"They know nothing," she quickly whispers. "They just act as if they know. He hasn't written to them a single letter," she gasps. "Please, go. It's my job to escort you out, but you should know they know nothing." She looks at me with her black eyes, startled.

"Thanks," I briefly touch her palm, which is firmly holding the closed door's handle. "Thank you," I'm gasping too. "Let's get out of here," I say to Grace.

"Try the Ministry of Defense. Maybe they know something," the maid runs after us and quietly says as we walk out the front door.

"Thank you," I say to her, once again, and quickly walk towards the iron gate, crossing it and looking at the wall, the American flag, and the Morelli name etched into a white marble slab next to the black gate.

"Francesca, what are you doing?" Grace yells when she notices that I'm holding a delicate Chinese vase that was standing in the foyer, "Francesca, why did you take it?" She's trying to hold my hand as I raise it and forcibly throw the Chinese vase at the marble slab carrying the family name, watching as it shatters into a thousand pieces and scatters in the street.

"American flag?" I turn and scream at her as I point to the Star-spangled banner that flutters lightly in the afternoon breeze. "American flag? The members of this family were fascists. They wore black uniforms and did the Nazi salute. The men in this family came to my wedding dressed in black uniforms," I continue to shout in the street, ignoring a car that passes by while the driver looks at me. "This family supported Hitler. I wouldn't be surprised if Mussolini hosted parties here. And now they're friends of the Americans? Now they host Americans in their guest room?" I spit in the direction of the gate.

"Let's go, Francesca." Grace comes over and hugs me. "Let's go to the Ministry of Defense. Maybe they know something."

"This is Italy here. Nobody knows anything. Only women are looking for their husbands here. Nobody else cares," I wipe my tears.

"Let's go. Surely someone there could help us," she keeps hugging me.

"I'm sorry, I can't help you," says the American officer sitting behind the mahogany desk at the Ministry of Defense, the same desk in front of which I once sat opposite an Italian clerk in a suit.

The man who was here before is gone, and so are all the employees around him, replaced by American soldiers in khaki uniforms. The large shelves at the back of the hall, which were full of documents, are now also empty, and all the women who sat near the teleprinter machines have disappeared. Only the brown chairs they sat on remained next to the silent metal machines.

"Please, I have to know," I say and write Emanuele's name and unit on a piece of paper, giving it to him.

"I'm sorry," he awkwardly smiles and doesn't take the piece of paper. "Everything that was here was taken. I don't even know where they took it, maybe to Washington," he looks at Grace, who sits next to me. "The Intelligence has taken everything from here," he moans. "I can't help you, Mrs. Morelli."

"Please, sir, you're my only hope," I place the paper on the desk, in front of him.

"One moment," Grace takes the paper, folds it, takes out a stack of bills and places it inside, pushes it toward him on the table. "We have to know, and I'm a soldier in your army. Please, help me."

The officer sighs, takes the folded paper, walks away, and disappears into the back room.

He must know. He must find something. There must be a piece of information, someone who knows something.

My fingers scratch the table's wooden surface, trying to peel it off.

"Mrs. Morelli, I'm sorry," he returns after a few minutes and puts the paper on the table, once again sitting before me. "I don't know anything specific, but your husband's probably been killed. I'm sorry," he pushes the folded paper towards me, and I see that all the money is still there.

"I don't believe you," I whisper, feeling Grace's hand on my arm.

"I'm sorry. It's impossible to know exactly what happened to him. Only the Russians may know, but it's likely that he was killed, and even if he were captured as a prisoner of war, he probably didn't survive."

"Thank you," Grace says to him and stands up, holding my hand, but I let go and stay seated.

"I only had one husband I loved, and you took him to war. I don't care if it's you or whoever was sitting here before you," I raise my voice. "How could it be that he's gone?" I shout, ignoring the people around, who raise their heads and look at me, but I can no longer hold back.

"Mrs. Morelli, it's not us..." he tries to answer.

"I don't care who it is, whether it's the Germans, the Italians, the Russians or you. You all look the same with your clean, ironed uniforms and polite smiles. You conquered us, so you're responsible now. I want my husband. I want someone to bring me my husband back. He went to war, and his trace was lost, and no one can tell me what happened to him," I scream through my tears and crumple the piece of paper bearing his name that was left on the table.

"Please, Mrs. Morelli..." I notice more soldiers standing

around me, feeling Grace's hand trying to hold me.

"Someone, just give me my husband back, please..." I whimper.

"Mrs. Morelli..." I can see through my tears that he's playing with the pen in his fingers. His eyes are also red. "I'm so sorry..."

"You have nothing to be sorry for. I'm the one wearing a black dress..." I try to calm myself as he signals to the people standing around us that they can return to their desks.

"Maybe the Russians know something, but they're not telling us anything."

"And how do I get to the Russians?" I wipe my nose and eyes.

"It's impossible to get to Russia now. Maybe when the war is over, but even then, you probably won't be able to find him," he leans forward, takes out a handkerchief from the pocket of his military jacket, and hands it to me. "And no one will ever let you cross the border into Russia."

"Let's get out of here," I stand up and hold Grace's hand as I wipe away my tears. "Let's get out of this cursed city."

※

Two months later, as I ride my motorcycle across the hospital's ruined iron gate, I look around and slam the breaks.

The hospital's front driveway is full of military trucks, parked near the entrance, and their back ramps opened. I park my bike at the side, near the pile of gasoline barrels, and watch the soldiers going out of the building, carrying equipment, and loading the trucks.

"Miss, can you move your bike a little?" A soldier asks me. He and his friend are loading the heavy barrels onto one of the trucks; they all remove their shirts, and their sweaty skins glisten in the morning sun. What's happening here?

Inside the hospital, the corridor on the second floor is full of wooden crates placed one on top of the other, and soldiers are taking them down to the entrance hall. Where is Grace?

"Are you leaving?" I approach and ask as I notice her standing next to the bed of a wounded soldier, changing his bandage.

"I'm sorry," she doesn't look at me and continues to cut the used bandage that's wrapped around his hand.

"You're sorry? When did you think of telling me?" I take the used bandage from her hand and throw it into the stainless-steel bucket beside us.

"It's new. It's not like I knew about it and hid it from you," she looks at me.

"How new?"

"Francesca, the war is moving forward. The Germans are retreating. We both know that the hospital has to move north. It's a military hospital."

"Don't call me Francesca," I say to her as the soldier whose bandage she's changing looks at me curiously. "I'm called the 'stupid Italian,' the one no one tells they're about to leave here."

"Francesca, we're friends," she hugs me for a moment and returns to bandage the soldier, who keeps looking at us.

"But you're leaving."

"I'm sorry, but the war has wandered north, and we're

military forces. We're going wherever they send us."

"I thought we were friends. You can wander back to America, you, and your wounded," I look at him, and he stops smiling. "And give me back my orange tree that your tank ran over when you came to my village," I turn to walk away from her. She could've told me they were leaving and not surprise me like that.

"Francesca..." I hear her from behind, but I walk faster, so she can't catch up with me with her limp and go out of the building. I pass the hospital's garden on the way to my spot and look around. There're less wounded in the hospital, and only a few of them are sitting in the white chairs spread around the garden, enjoying the morning sun. It's only at my spot, behind the old shed, that I sit down and look at the tall cypress trees surrounding me. Soon the war will be over, and I'll be alone with my child, wearing a black dress. I shouldn't have let her be my friend.

"I should've told you." She stands over me a few minutes later. "But I thought it was good news for you too. The war will soon be over."

"You can't decide what's good for me," I look up at her. I once had a friend who chose the Germans' side and disappeared, and now she'll leave me too.

"You don't have to be so nasty."

"Did you forget that I'm the Italian woman who hates everyone? You shouldn't have become my friend," I say and regret the words after a moment.

"Maybe it's a good thing we're getting out of here. I won't have to hear any more of your complaints about the American army occupying you," she raises her voice at me.

"I shouldn't have put the statue of Saint Mary under your

mattress to protect you," I say, even though I don't mean it.

"I didn't heal because of you or your Saint Mary," she shouts at me. "I recovered thanks to American doctors, American sulfa powder, and American morphine," she throws a pack of cigarettes my way. "And by the way, all the cigarettes you ask for or steal from me are American," she turns and slowly limps away.

"I'm sorry. I'm glad that Saint Mary looked after you," I still manage to shout after her, but she doesn't turn around and continues walking away. I'm debating whether to take out one of the cigarettes and smoke them or keep the box closed and put it in my hiding place under the bed later. I have to go to her and apologize.

In the following days, the army trucks keep arriving and loading equipment, and the corridors of the mansion that used to be a hospital are becoming empty. Still, I don't go over to talk to her, trying not to look up as I keep scrubbing the floor every morning, so that I don't accidentally see her. I'll miss her.

The ambulances and jeeps that park outside at the front driveway are also disappearing, and every evening, as I walk to my motorcycle, I look at the emptied parking lot. "They won't care if I'll take some," I say to myself as I fill a jerrycan of fuel from the few barrels left and tie it to my bike. I'll soon need it.

"Francesca, someone is waiting for you outside," Mom says to me a few days later, and I go to the front door and see who it is.

"I was told I'd find you here," she stands in the street and looks at me.

"Yes, I'm here," I walk down the stone steps towards her. I no longer work at the hospital as of yesterday. The nurse in charge called me and relieved me of my duties, politely shaking my hand.

"It took me a long time to find your house," she says, still looking at me.

"You must've asked about the stupid Italian woman, and they didn't know what to answer."

"No, I asked about the Italian woman with the motorcycle, but it took me a while to find someone who spoke English."

"So, this is where I live, in this alley," I point around at the simple stone buildings and the narrow street.

"What is this?" She points to a stain of red paint that's been painted on the cobblestones of the street outside the small wooden shed.

"I don't know," I don't want to tell her about Gabriele and the red I'd painted where he lay that night. He died because of me.

"I came to say goodbye," she awkwardly sways.

"I know. Come inside."

"No, no, I'm in a hurry. I need to go. They're already waiting for me, but I brought you something," she hands me a small package wrapped in paper. "Open it after I leave."

"Thanks," I'm holding the package and looking for something to say to her, but she's already giving me a little smile, turns around and limps away.

"Grace," I shout after a moment and run towards her, removing the small cross from my neck and giving it to her. "Saint Mary will always watch over you."

"Thank you," she holds the delicate necklace, and I notice her red eyes. "Don't forget, open it only after I leave," she keeps walking and disappears into the alley. I wait for a few moments before I tear off the brown wrapping paper on her gift and see an Italian-Russian dictionary.

Red Army Archive
November 2021, Kyiv, Ukraine

Anna

"Certificates," the clerk at the entrance of the large concrete building looks at us indifferently while Natasha and I stand in front of her. We remove our gloves and hand her our IDs. "Why did you come?" She asks after glancing at our cards.

"We're looking for information on World War II."

"Basement floor, second wing," she gives us back our IDs and turns to look at the TV screen on the wall. In the news studio, two commentators are debating whether the Russians will try to attack Kyiv or not. That's the only thing they've been talking about for several months now. I look away from the TV screen and put my IDs back in my purse, rubbing my hands together to warm up as we both go down the concrete steps and stand in front of the locked glass door; I ring the bell.

"I see that you're writing a paper about the period after the Stalingrad battles ended," the archive employee says as she looks at the letter she's holding.

"Yes," We both answer, sitting before her desk.

"Is it an academic paper?" She keeps looking at the paper bearing the official university seal, signed by the head of the faculty.

"Yes," we nod and say nothing else. On the way there, we agreed that we'd talk as little as possible as to avoid any confusion or embarrassment should they find out that we weren't actually history students.

"And are you interested in receiving the German prisoners of war list in the Bektovka POW camp from February 1943?" She keeps asking.

"The Italian POWs," I correct her.

"There was no separation between them," she replies. "Wait there," she points to the tables on the side of the hall and picks up the phone, still holding the letter from the university in her hand. Where is she calling?

"Do you think she believed us?" Natasha whispers as we walk towards the large tables on the side of the hall and sit down. The archivist on the phone and two other people are the only ones other than us in the large room, most of which is filled with rows upon rows of shelves containing closed, gray cardboard boxes.

"We tried our best," I whisper back, even though the three archivists are at the other end of the hall and can't hear us. I follow the archive employee with my look as she puts down the black phone's handset, gets up from her desk, and walks towards us, holding the paper we gave her. Did she check if we were history students at the university?

"Do you only want the list of prisoners of the Bektovka camp or all other camps in southern Russia as well?"

"How many prisoners of war are we talking about?" Natasha asks her.

"About one hundred thousand Germans and Italian soldiers."

"Only the Bektovka camp then," I quickly reply. Even so, we hardly have any chance of locating him. We have his last name at best, that's all. And maybe grandma told me the truth, and he died in the snow in the ruins of Stalingrad.

"Wait here for a few minutes," she tells us. "You can make yourselves tea or coffee while you wait," she points to the stainless-steel samovar standing on a table, in the corner of the room. "It'll take some time."

"There you go, Bektovka POW camp, February-September 1943," one of the employees brings several large cardboard notebooks to our table and places them in front of us.

I open the first notebook and look at the endless list of names written in neat handwriting, line under line, page after page.

"What's the letter G?" I ask him. Next to each name is their rank, identity number, and an additional letter.

"G – German," he replies.

"And Italian?" Natasha asks him.

"It," he replies.

"And what are the lines on the names?" I ask him. A straight, red line is drawn by pen over many of the names.

"These didn't survive the camp," he looks at me.

"Thank you," I say to him and examine the large, old notebooks lying on the table. "Let's get started," I say to Natasha as he walks away from us, and we divide the notebooks between us. "We'll only look for Italians under the name Morelli. Maybe we'll find something."

"I found it," Natasha whispers after some time, and I put down the notebook in my hand and look at her finger. She found him. I approach her and watch the surname Morelli written in rounded letters. He has a Sergeant rank and a straight, red line across it.

"Would you like another cup of tea?" I get up from my chair. Maybe this whole search for a dead man is stupid.

"Yes," she also gets up from her chair and stretches, and

we walk towards the samovar on the table in the corner.

Ninety minutes later, I find another Morelli, this one survived. And at the end of the day, when we close the last notebook and thank the woman in charge of the archive, we have a list of four Italian prisoners named Morelli. Two with a red pen line across their names and two who left the camp alive.

"You have to talk to your grandmother," Natasha says as we leave the archive and walk towards the tram, wearing our coats. It started snowing again.

"I'll stop by her house tomorrow," I say, the palm of my gloved hand tucked into my pocket, touching the paper with the four names written on it.

"Would you like me to join you?"

"No, I want to go to her alone," I reply, although she deserves an invitation. "But I promise you I'll go straight back to the dorm and tell you what she said," I put my arm in hers as we walk in the snow. I want to hear grandma's story by myself, to know how the story ends and who the woman in the picture is.

"I hope he's not dead," she says as we wait at the station, moving from side to side to keep warm.

"Me too," I quietly say as the street lantern turns on.

"Grandma, I have to know," I say to her the next day as soon as I enter her house and hang my coat on the coat rack.

"How are you, Anuchka?" She hugs me, and I can smell from her hands the sweet Oludashki waiting for me.

"I'm fine. Please tell me."

"I thought you'd come yesterday," she moves away from me a little. "I was waiting for you. Did you have a lot of courses at university?"

"I found his name."

"Whose name?" She looks at me.

"Her man's name," I go to the display case, reach out, take the key, and open the glass doors.

"Anuchka, what are you doing?"

"You have to tell me if I'm right," I take the photo from the wooden box, even though she'd probably be angry with me. "I found her man's name," I hold up the picture and take out the list of names written on the piece of paper, handing it to her. "Please tell me who he was."

"I don't understand," Grandma holds the paper in her trembling fingers and looks at it, walks to the small table at the side of the room, takes her reading glasses, and looks at the paper again. "What are these names?" She sits down on the sofa, holding the paper and the photo of the woman standing by the motorcycle. "Anuchka, what is this?"

"Did you meet an Italian soldier in the war? Did he give you the picture? Was he a prisoner of war? What was his name?" I can't stop asking her questions. I have to know.

She doesn't answer me, just looks at the list and sighs, takes off her glasses for a moment, rubs her eyes, and puts them back on.

"I don't even know what his name was," she finally says, placing the list of names on the small table. "It's so stupid, but I never thought to ask him for his name."

"And why didn't you ever tell me about him?" I sit down next to her and hug her.

"Because some things that aren't meant to be told."

"Why, grandma? I'm all grown up. I have to know," I keep hugging her.

"Because I wanted to love him so much," she replies after some time. "And I so wanted him to live, and I didn't want anyone to know. You see, my Anuchka, sometimes the past and what we did is too complicated that you don't want to talk about it."

"Did you love an Italian prisoner of war?"

"No, my Anuchka, I loved a man with a sad look in his eyes, but it was forbidden," she hands me the picture with her shaking hands. "And all that time, I knew there must have been someone else who loved him more and didn't know whether he was dead or alive."

The Road to Russia
Italy, September 1945, five months after the war ended

Francesca

"Enough, Mom," I finish praying and stand up in my small room, crossing myself in front of the Holy Mary statuette hanging on the wall. She will protect me like she kept Grace alive while she was under her hospital mattress. I open my eyes and stand in front of my wooden wardrobe.

"You can't do it," Mom says, standing at the door and watching me.

"I have to." I open the closet and look at my clothes. I'll have to settle for my black dress and a few more items. I grab one simple camisole, a few pairs of underwear, a bra, and a coat, and throw them on my bed. I need my coat, even though it's old and torn.

"How will we manage without you?"

"You'll be fine." I hug her for a moment before I turn back and start stuffing the clothes that I threw on the bed into my leather backpack. "You know I left most of what I had in the jar hidden in the kitchen."

"I know. Still, there aren't any jobs around."

"Mom, please leave." I turn to her.

"Why? What are you going to do?"

"Please, go out."

"I nursed you when you were a baby. You don't need to hide things from me," she says, but leaves the room. I close the door behind her and rush to my bed, pull out the sharp knife I keep under my pillow and insert it into my boot. It'll protect me.

"What did you do?" She returns a few minutes later and examines the room to see what has changed.

"Nothing." I straighten my dress.

"I know you're a married and faithful woman, but you barely knew him."

"Five years ago, I took a vow in church 'only death will do us part' and indeed only death will separate us." I bend down, pull out the cardboard box from under my bed, take out all the cigarette boxes I've collected over the past few months, and stuff them into a burlap sack. I'll need them for the ride since I'm not taking any money.

"You have a child!"

"Yes, I have a child." I fight the urge to cry. "I know I have a child." I hope she won't notice my tears under the oil lamp's dim light. "And this child needs a father." Raffaele is asleep in his small bed in the corner of the room; he's lying on his back and breathing peacefully.

"Enough, Francesca, enough of that," she grabs the backpack on the bed and pours out its contents. "I'm putting these things back in the closet. You're not going."

"Mom, let it go." I grasp the leather strap of the backpack tightly, pulling it towards me.

"You know Emanuele is dead." She messily shoves my things into the closet and raises her voice. "I apologize for saying this, but you know it's true. How many men have returned to the village since the war ended?" She shuts the closet door and leans on it. "None! I'm not letting you go."

"Mom, you'll wake him up."

"Maybe he should wake up to see his mother leaving him."

"Enough, mother! I have to go. Maybe he's still alive in

Russia." I try to move her aside by force and start crying. "You know they take prisoners of war, and they don't release them. They're not like the Americans."

"You don't know that, and neither do I. All I only know is that you have a child and you're leaving him in order to go to Russia. You know that he didn't survive." She pushed back, leaning with all her might against the closet door. "And I know that if you have a child, you do not leave him behind."

"I'll leave with or without my clothes. You'd do the same if you were me. You also went looking for Dad."

"No, I didn't. I should have stopped him from going to these demonstrations. What good is it to me that he's dead? And now you're going to die too."

"I'll be back. I promise." I feel the tears rolling my face. She's crying too. "Please, let me go."

She moves aside without saying a word and opens the closet door. I hug her, feeling her body's warmth and her arms around me.

"I have to go," I say a few moments later. I start repacking my backpack. If I don't leave now, I won't have the courage to go at all. I take his leather jacket off the hanger and smell it before I put it on, but after all these years, most of the scent faded. His smell disappeared long ago. "I'll be back soon." I hug her one last time and put the backpack over my shoulder.

"Wait," Mom says. She takes down the small statuette of Saint Mary and puts it in my backpack. "At least she'll look after you."

"Thank you." I head to the front door.

"What about him? Won't you say goodbye to him?"

"I don't want him to wake up and cry." I turn my back to her, so she won't see my tears. I can't bear the thought of leaving him behind. I grab the handle and open the door, but before I head out I turn around, go over to Raffaele's bed, lean over and kiss him. "Goodbye, my son. I promise to be back soon," I whisper to him over and over, feeling Mom's hand on my shoulder and seeing my teardrops forming round stains on his cream-colored pajamas. I have to go.

"Come back soon." Mom hugs me for a long time before I close the door behind me and hurry down the alley. I don't look back, so I won't change my mind.

My red motorcycle awaits me in the shed. I've tied another jerrycan of fuel to its side. I shove the burlap sack with the cigarette packs into the motorcycle's other side bag. I left most of the money I had to Mom and Raffaele.

Don't think about what you're about to do, don't change your mind. I have a husband who I had vowed to love till death. I have to know what happened to him.

I zip the leather jacket, feeling the map folded in the inside pocket, the same map of Europe I once took from the head nurse's desk and marked the Russian border on it. But borders have no meaning anymore. The war was over, and they won. Europe belongs to them and the Americans; not to women such as me who had lost their husbands.

I kick the starter pedal, and the motorcycle roars to life, filling the night silence of the village with a loud ticking sound. I didn't want to leave during the day so that Raffaele wouldn't see me driving away.

I wipe away my tears for the last time and squeeze the throttle and slowly drive through the dark on the cobblestones, with nothing but the light of the street lanterns showing me the way. They've started lighting some of them again. I take one last look at the stone steps leading home and the red stain marked on the pavement. In the dark, it looks almost black. I drive quickly to the village exit. I'll drive a few hours tonight before I stop to sleep.

"Where are you headed?" An American soldier asks me four days later at a military roadblock on the Austrian-Hungarian border. He approaches me slowly, walking through the muddy dirt road in a khaki tarpaulin cape coat glistening in the rain.

"To visit my mother. She lives in Budapest," I say to him still sitting on my rattling motorcycle. My hips ache from the long ride, and my body is shivering. The rain's been falling since the early morning and I'm soaking wet. My coat is completely drenched in water and isn't exactly helpful against the cold. I hope I'll soon find a place to hide until it warms up a bit and the rain stops.

"Do you know that you're about to leave the American occupation zone and enter the Russian army zone?" He raises his voice over my bike's rattling, and I nod, wiping the raindrops from my face with my cold hand.

"Have a good ride," he nonchalantly says as he lifts the wooden barrier, waiting for me to drive through so he can return to his small wooden shack. The Stars and Stripes flag hoisted on top of the shack is dripping with water. Only a hundred feet of muddy road stands between the American occupation zone and the Russian zone. I can still change my mind and turn around.

"Where are you going?" The soldier at the next roadblock asks me in Russian, shouting from the opening of the small shack. He has a submachine gun carelessly hanging on his shoulder.

"To Budapest, to mother," I reply, hoping I've pronounced the words correctly in Russian.

"Documents," he shouts back.

"There you go." I take out two packs of cigarettes from my coat pocket and show them to him.

"Your documents aren't good enough." He stares at me and places his hand on his submachine gun.

"There you go, I've got better documents." I take out two more cigarette packs from my coat pocket and show them to him as well.

He walks towards me in the rain, indifferently stepping into a puddle, takes the cigarettes, and signals me to enter the Russian occupied territory. Now I can no longer turn around and go back. I mustn't think about it. I gently squeeze the throttle, and the motorcycle travels down the muddy road through the tall trees surrounding me. I'll probably find a place to stop soon.

The bullet-riddled road sign attached to a wooden post on the side of the road announces: **170 Miles to Budapest**. Someone has painted the words **862 Miles to Kyiv, 1371 Miles to Stalingrad** in big red letters.

"Take this, have some soup. It'll warm you up." He stands next to me and hands me a steaming stainless-steel bowl.

"Thanks." I smile at him as I take the bowl, feeling it warm up my frozen hands. I look at the group of refugees sitting around the fire on the side of the road leading from

Budapest to the east. The military roadblock and the soldier at the Russian occupation zone entrance seem like a distant memory. Since then, I've passed more barriers, crossing them with the help of packs of cigarettes. The village, Mom, and Raffaele also seem so far away amidst the dark trees surrounding me.

"What's your next destination?" I ask him and wipe a tear away.

"Are you okay?" He sits beside me, soup bowl in hand, occasionally sipping slowly.

"Yes, everything is fine," I smile at him and wipe away another tear. He's the only one in the group who speaks a little Italian. The others speak only Polish, and some also speak Russian, of which I understand a couple of words.

I met them earlier this evening when I was looking for a place to rest my head for the night, perhaps an abandoned shed or a barn. But then I saw their bonfire, and they invited me to eat and spend the night with them.

"We're on our way to Austria. Then, we'll continue to Italy," he answers and blows on his hot soup.

"You have a long way to go." I look at the people gathered around the bonfire. The men and women sit in silence or talk quietly to each other, and the only sound ringing through the air is their dishes clinking from time to time. The handful of children here don't run and laugh as children should. They sit and eat in silence with the grownups, dressed in coats that are too large for them. One of the men's arms is exposed, and I notice a number branded on his hand.

"He came from those camps," the man sitting next to me says when he notices me staring.

"And how about you?" I ask. The newspapers started reporting stories about these camps only after the war ended. I've never met someone who was imprisoned in one of those camps.

"Me too," he says quietly. "A long time ago, before the war, I was a doctor in Vienna. I had a wife, Adela, and two children, Franz, and Jacob." I stay silent, reluctant to ask what had happened to them. I read about those camps in the newspapers.

"And them?" I look at the children.

"They survived somehow, but they're orphans. We all survived somehow." He doesn't say anything else. "And how about you?" He asks me after a while.

"I'm on my way to Russia." I grasp for the right words. What would he think of me if he knew my husband was a soldier in the Italian army fighting alongside the Germans? Will he regret sharing his soup with me and inviting me to spend the night with them? "I'm looking for my husband. I want to know what happened to him."

"Is he in Russia?"

"I don't know where he is anymore. He was in Russia three years ago."

"He must have survived somehow." He puts his hand on my shoulder when he notices that I'm shaking.

"I'm sure he did," I answer with a trembling voice and sip my soup.

"Be careful when you arrive at the border checkpoint to Russia."

"I've already passed military roadblocks on my way." I look at a little boy lying on the ground in front of the fire; his eyes are shut. He's a little older than my Raffaele, maybe just by a year or two. "I know how to manage at checkpoints," I add. I've used my little cigarette stash at every checkpoint, I've even given a couple to the mechanic who repaired my motorcycle a few days ago.

"The next checkpoint is different. It's not the like the others," he says quietly, and I turn my gaze to him, noticing his blue eyes sparkling in the fire's light. "This isn't just any checkpoint, manned by a drunken Russian soldier. This is the border line to Russia, to Stalin's communism, and Stalin doesn't like guests. It's dangerous to go in, and it is almost impossible to get out." He looks at me.

"Were you there?"

"No. I was in Poland in a place called Auschwitz." He pauses for a moment before continuing. "But some of them," he glances at the other people, "were there, in Russia."

"I'll be fine," I say. I need to sleep and be ready for tomorrow.

"Don't tell anyone that you're Italian. They hate the Germans and the Italians," he adds when he gets up and adds his empty soup bowl to the pile of dishes before he walks away and blurts a "good night," at my direction.

"Farewell," I stand beside my motorcycle early on the next morning and say goodbye to the doctor. The other people I spent the night with are packing their belongings, rolling their simple army woolen blankets into bundles, and tying them together.

"Good luck," he shakes my hand.

"Thanks, good luck to you too." I shiver in the chilly air, looking at the fog surrounding us. "Take it." I pull out a few packs of cigarettes from my burlap bag and give them to him, "for the road."

"Thanks, but you'll need them more than I will," he refuses to take them.

"Please, let me give you something in return." I insist, even though I have almost none left, and he holds them and smiles at me.

"May God protect you," I hear him saying when I start my motorcycle, and the engine disturbs the silence, piercing through the morning frosty air.

"May the Jewish God watch over you." I wave goodbye to him and start driving slowly, thinking that maybe they and I have the same God.

The sides of the road are spotted with remains of German military vehicles. Some have been flipped over, as if pushed off the road by a tractor, and some are riddled with bullet holes. Only the Nazi black cross on the vehicle's body suggests that they had once belonged to the undefeated German army that plowed through here on its way to conquer the world.

'To the Soviet Union Border.' I drive past a road sign with an arrow pointing forward. I quickly drive ahead on the ruined and winding road through the forest and the German armored vehicles on the sides. A few hours later, after sunrise, I notice it in the distance and stop my motorcycle.

The red flag with the hammer and sickle is hoisted above the guard post and the barracks, waving gently in the afternoon breeze. I stay on my motorcycle and examine them from a safe distance. Will they let me cross the border? I have a few cigarette boxes, no documents or money to give them.

I make a snap decision and throw the fuel jerrycan

attached to the side of my bike. It's empty anyways and does nothing but shake noisily as I drive. I glance at the guard post one last time and turn my motorcycle into a side dirt road. They won't let me pass. I'll bypass the checkpoint, like I did in Italy.

The dirt road is muddy, and I drive slowly through the tall trees, looking for the right path that will lead me past the Russian border. But then, the road takes a sharp turn and I find myself facing a military motorcycle and two soldiers standing beside it. One of them raises his weapon and aims it at me.

"Stop the engine." The taller of the two signals at me. Even though I want to speed up and run away on the muddy road, I know they'll shoot me. Did I make a mistake?

Silence falls when I turn the engine off, and I can hear the birds chirping in the trees, the leaves rustling in the breeze, and the sound of the bootsteps of the soldier approaching me.

He's wide and dressed in a simple green uniform. His submachine gun is still pointed at me as he approaches with a big smile. I notice he has one missing tooth.

"Documents," he says in Russian. I can smell the vodka on his breath.

"There you go," I reply in Russian and slowly lean to the side, intending to take out the cigarette boxes I have left and give them to him.

"Are you Russian?" He yells at me and slightly pokes my belly with the submachine gun's barrel.

"No, Hungarian," I reply, looking into his eyes. What have I done? I want to scream.

"What do you have there?" He points the barrel at my hand tucked into the burlap sack.

"Certificates." It might work. This is my only chance. I must stay calm.

"Take your hand out."

I pull out the cigarette boxes and hand them to him. "Certificates." Did I do the right thing? How will he react?

"American cigarettes." He laughs out loud and turns to his friend, holding the boxes and showing him. "Nyet Hungarian." He turns to me. "Nyet Communist, you're a capitalist." He spits on the mud and thrusts the submachine gun barrel into my stomach again.

"Nyet Capitalist," I reply and look into his eyes. "Hungarian Bolshevik."

Breathe slowly, keep calm, do not make any sharp movements.

The metal barrel seems to burn my stomach. *Do not look down. Keep looking into his eyes.*

"Raise your hands," he signals with his head and gun barrel. I slowly raise my hands and frantically look at him and at the other soldiers, his weapon also pointed at me. All I can hear are the birds tweeting around. The soldier's missing tooth suddenly seems so prominent.

His outstretched hand quickly unzips my leather jacket, and I can feel his fingers groping me, touching my breasts, squeezing them before continuing his search.

"Capitalist spy," he pulls the map out of my jacket and shows it to his friend. "Enemy," he says to the other soldier, who approaches and looks at the map, then turns to me and spits on the motorcycle.

"Nyet Capitalist, Hungarian," I keep repeating. I must stick to my story, and I mustn't make any mistakes, but all I want to do is scream

"Italian," says his friend, pointing to the route I had

marked on the map. "Italian and German are the same."

"Nyet," I say to him.

What should I do? My hands start to tremble.

"Shut up," the big soldier shouts at me, his fingers close around my neck, and he pulls my face closer to him. He reeks of vodka. "You, come with us."

"Okay." I nod as he releases my neck. I breathe again and cough. What are their intentions? They walk a few feet away and talk to each other, but I can't hear a thing.

"Follow us," the other soldier says and climbs on his motorcycle. I nod and start my motorcycle. I'll escape as soon as we get out of this muddy road and the opportunity presents itself. But then the big soldier approaches and climbs my motorcycle, holding me from behind. "Follow him," he laughs again as his huge hands clutch my breasts.

Do as they say, I'll find a solution. Don't panic. Ignore the soldier pressed against you and his disgusting hands. I'll be fine. I always find a way. Now concentrate on driving.

My hands grip the motorcycle handles tightly, careful not to slip on the muddy path, and we drive through the serpentine road and the trees until I spot the border checkpoint around the bend; the same one I tried to avoid.

The guard post is surrounded by barbed wire fences, and at the bullet-pierced sign on the right states 'Halt' in German. The abandoned car next to it is also riddled with bullets.

There's one guard post, and a shed or wheat barn behind it, there's also a Russian sergeant, and two soldiers standing and watching us as we approach them. 'Stop,' he gestures.

"Who is she?" The sergeant seems to be asking the soldier parking their motorcycle.

"Capitalist Italian." The big soldier laughs as he grabs

my arm and pulls me off my bike, and I hold back from screaming in pain. I must be obedient until I get my chance to escape.

"Should we report her?" The soldier asks the sergeant, who smilingly approaches and stands close to me. He's thinner than the others and has a black mustache.

"No," he answers a few seconds later. "We'll keep her here." He examines me. "Don't report her." He shouts to the soldier standing at the guard post and holding the field telephone's handset. Why don't they want to report me? Will they let me go?

"And what about Nikolai?" The large soldier reeking of vodka asks.

"He could be the first one," the sergeant replies. "Then we'll have our share." He laughs, and the others join him. This is my chance. I push the big man on the sergeant and kick him as hard as I can, quickly turning around and running towards the motorcycle. But then I see one of the soldiers sitting on it and gulping down a bottle of vodka. I stand there, panting and looking at him and at my motorcycle. I failed.

"Capitalist bitch," I feel a hand pulling on my hair. I let out a scream, trying to resist him while the big soldier drags me by my hair towards the barn on the side of the road. The soldiers start guffawing when he throws me into the barn and slams the wooden door behind.

The Border Checkpoint
September 1945, Hungary – USSR border

Francesca

My hand tightly grips the knife I pulled out from my boot, and my eyes are fixed on the closed barn door. They'll soon open it and enter. I must be ready.

I hear their laughter outside and the noise of my motorcycle from time to time. They must be driving it in front of the checkpoint, but it doesn't matter anymore. I did my best, and now I must concentrate on the door and be ready.

I pass the knife to my other hand and wipe my sweaty palm on my black dress, dry my fingers and return the knife to my strong hand; the blade mustn't slip when I attack. I'll only have one shot when they come in. However, I know I'll never leave this barn alive. Still, I don't think about it. They won't get me without a fight. They won't get me at all.

I can hear the sound of a jeep approaching outside, and my motorcycle engine stops rattling, as well as the soldiers laughing and talking.

Should I get closer to the door, try to peek, and see what they're doing outside? Or should I wait in the dark and try to hide in that haystack in the corner? Maybe I should get closer to the door and surprise them when they enter? I step back into the corner. I'll try and hide, but then the door opens, and I watch him. He looks at me too.

He's wearing an officer's cap with a red star in its center, and his green uniform looks cleaner than the other soldiers.

The brown leather belt on his pants is worn out, as is the leather holster on his waist. He's probably an officer who went through the war and not one of those new recruits they'd drafted to fill the gaps. Will I be able to surprise him? How experienced is he?

I try to look down and examine his holster without him noticing. If I can just get to his gun, I might get out of here alive, but he's watching me, and I look at him, studying his clean-shaven face and dark eyes. He doesn't scare me. I won't look down.

"I'm next," I hear a laugh from outside, or at least this is what I think one of the soldiers is saying, and I manage to notice them through the barn entrance. I won't get out of here alive.

He watches me for a moment, steps back, shouts something that I can't understand to the soldiers, and closes the door, leaving us alone in the filthy barn. I have to lower my gaze, so he'd think I'm afraid of him. At least I have the knife I'm hiding in my hand.

He cautiously approaches me and examines me, looking down at my dress and legs. His eyes go up, and he looks at mine.

Now!

I spit at him, and he backs off for a second. I quickly stretch my knife-holding hand, aim the blade at his neck, but he moves back, and his hand rises and forcefully holds on to mine. I scream in pain as he bends my hand, and the knife drops.

Don't give up!

I hear another scream, but it seems to come from my own mouth as he slaps me hard, and I lose my balance. Still, I try to grab him and reach for his gun with my other hand.

My fingers slide over the soft leather, and I scream again as he pushes me to the barn floor, and I only have the scattered straw to soften my fall.

"Shout," he whispers to me in Russian while standing over me, watching. "Shout."

Breathe, breathe. Don't give up. It doesn't matter anymore.

I look around, searching for my knife, but can't find it on the dirty barn floor covered in scattered straw. I raise my eyes, notice his hand gently caressing his holster. How bad will he hurt me?

"Shout," he whispers to me again, this time in Italian. But the words sound strange to me in his thick Russian accent.

I look at him and examine his black eyes again, making sure to look directly at them while my hand gently rummages through the hay, trying to locate the knife, I have to make subtle movements so he won't notice. I have to smile at him.

"My name is Nikolai Matveevich Berezovsky," he slowly says in bad Italian, standing over me, his hand resting on his holster. I keep looking at him and don't say a thing. "Shout," he continues to say to me, but I remain silent, waiting for him to lean over me so I can blind him with my nails. I won't give him the pleasure of hearing me scream. "I'm an officer in the 38th Red Soviet Army," he keeps saying.

My hand freezes as I notice he sees me searching through the hay. He's not stupid. I have to smile at him. "I enlisted on July 1941, when the war started, and I killed more Germans than I can count," he says and bends down, and I tense up. I won't have another chance. He already knows I'll try and hurt him. "And I've also killed too many Germans for me to forget," he grabs something on the floor and throws it at me, and I feel the butt of the knife hitting my thighs. "Shout," he continues to say to me, but I just watch him in silence, holding the knife he threw in my lap.

What does he want from me? Is he getting ready to shoot me? I hear the soldiers' laughter outside and the noise of the motorcycle that used to be mine.

"I once dreamed of becoming a physics teacher in Kyiv, where I grew up, even though it's difficult for a Jew like me to get into university," he continues to speak to me in bad Italian. Why is he talking to me? "Shout," he takes a pack of cigarettes out of his shirt pocket and looks at me. "They want to hear you scream," he says, and I watch him and remain silent, feeling the sweat on my knife-holding fingers. "When I was a teenager, I studied piano. I loved opera. I was sitting in the Kyiv opera house with my eyes closed, hearing the love stories playing on stage," he reaches out to me and offers me a cigarette, but I just keep looking into his eyes and shake my head 'no.' He'll hurt me. "You have to shout. They'll suspect something's wrong and come in. They want to hear you shout," he puts the pack of cigarettes back into the pocket of his military shirt and keeps watching me, getting a little closer, and I recoil and raise the knife at him. "I won't do anything to you. I won't rape you," he stops in his place.

"Why?" That's all I can ask him, even though these aren't the words I should say.

"Because I killed to protect my country, but I never raped. You see, I want one day to be able to play the piano again and listen to Italian opera without being ashamed of things I did," he quietly says to me. "But you have to shout now."

I gasp and try to say something, to shout, to make a sound, but a broken breath is the only thing that comes out, a weak whimper like that of a wounded animal. My mouth's dry, and I have to do something, so they don't enter.

"Please..." he kneels before me.

"Slap me," I whisper to him.

"What?"

"Slap me." I reach out to hold his hand, placing it on my cheek, feeling the warmth of his fingers. I have to shout.

He hits me in my face, and I feel the pain and close my eyes, but only a heavy breath comes out.

"Harder."

His palm stings my cheeks as if it was and iron rod searing my flesh, and I scream like a wounded animal, feeling the burst of tears running down my cheeks. I hear sounds of laughter through the closed wooden door.

"More," I whisper to him and continue to scream and whimper while closing my eyes, waiting for the next wave of pain that'll keep them outside the barn, and this time he hits me more gently.

"Sorry," I hear him through my tears and sobs. "I'm sorry."

I just keep wailing, ignore my tears and look into his dark eyes that watch me so closely.

"You shouldn't be in this place. You mustn't try to cross the border. It's too dangerous for you."

"I have a husband there."

"Where?"

"Over there, in Russia, a prisoner of war. I must find him."

"You won't find him. You need to go back."

"I have to," I wipe my tears, grabbing the knife once again.

"You won't make it. A few miles down the road, there's another checkpoint, and there're more of those on the roads, manned by Communist Party officers who look for the right kind of documents, searching for traitors. They'll stop you and won't show you mercy," he gets closer to me, maybe to hug me, but he notices my raised hand holding the knife and stops.

"He is my husband. I won't give up."

"He's dead, or he'll be back somehow. But if you cross the border, you'll die."

"I'm his wife," I whimper and feel the tears run down my chin and onto my black dress. "I am his wife..."

"Maybe he's a prisoner, maybe someone is taking care of him, but you won't be able to find him."

"I have to, I swore," I ignore the tears on my chin.

"Do you have children?" He keeps watching me.

"Yes, I have a child."

"Then go back to him. If you continue this way, you'll never see your child again."

"I can't give up."

"You must," he leans closer to me until I can smell his body odor, but he doesn't touch me.

"What will I do? How will I return from here?" I look at the door, "They're awaiting their turn."

He puts his hand on the leather holster and pulls the gun out, and I flinch back and want to scream, but once again, no words come out, just a low whimper.

"It's okay," he smiles at me and puts the gun in my hand. "It'll protect you. I took it from a German officer. I'll get myself another one."

I feel the cold, greasy metal pistol he puts in my hand, tighten my fingers on the gun's grip and look at the Nazi swastika engraved on it.

"We need to go out of here. They'll start to get suspicious," he whispers to me, and I look at him again, wiping away my tears. I have to listen to him.

"How?"

"The knife, you need to hide it. The gun too."

My fingers push the knife into my boot, but I can't manage

to insert the gun into my other one. I have to find a solution. They'll soon enter.

My fingers forcefully grab the hem of my dress, and I tear off a piece of it. I have to hurry. My hands tightly tie the cloth around my thighs and press the gun against my skin, ignoring the metal scratching me. It mustn't fall when I walk.

"Why are you doing this?" I watch him as I pull my dress down again.

"Are you ready?" He whispers to me, not answering my question.

"Yes," I nod.

"Forgive me for hurting you," he says, and I nod again.

His fingers grip my hair hard as he sets me up, and I scream, trying to get away from him, but he holds me tight and leads me out of the barn, whispering, "Shout."

I notice, through my teary eyes, the soldiers standing around my motorcycle and rummaging through my leather bag, scattering its contents everywhere. But when they see us, they turn around and smile, and one of them approaches us and reaches to grab my hand.

Nikolai continues to hold my hair hard, yells at him something in Russian that I can't understand and pushes him aside, continues to hold me tightly, this time by my arm, while leading me to the motorcycle.

The soldiers look at me and laugh at my limp, and I ignore the pain of the gun that wounds my inner thigh and feel the wetness of the blood running down my leg.

"What about us?" The soldier asks, but Nikolai continues pulling me to the motorcycle and shouts at him in Russian. I think I hear the words 'whore' and maybe even 'disease,' but I'm not sure.

The other soldiers leave the motorcycle, approach, and surround us, watch me. Still, Nikolai pushes them away with his shouts, and their hands only touch me for a moment, pinching my waist.

"Sick whore," he shouts at them. "Don't touch her," he spits on me to the sound of their laughter and continues to drag me to the motorcycle, and I scream and walk as fast as I can, feeling my cheek sore and wet from his saliva, but I don't bother to wipe it.

"Start your bike and get out of here," he whispers to me as he sits me down on the motorcycle, quickly gathers up my clothes thrown all around, and throws them into my backpack, placing it between my open thighs.

"Why?" I ask him as I hit my foot on the starter pedal, feel the engine roar to life, shudder under my aching thighs cling to it and feel the gun wound me.

"So that you always remember that there are good people on the other side as well," he whispers to me. "Get out of here," he shouts in Russian, and I push the accelerator, feel my motorcycle begin to move, still hearing the soldiers' curses being slowly swallowed up by the monotonous rumble of the engine leading me away from the Russian border. I try to keep myself steady on the dirt road and notice the bumps on the way, the tears in my eyes also disrupt my view.

"Holy Mary..." I walk through the forest, holding the Virgin's statue tightly in my hand. The border station is already far behind me. I mustn't think about what happened there or the soldiers' intentions. I have to concentrate on my prayer.

My motorcycle's parked by the side of the road, leaning on a destroyed tank - German or Russian, I no longer know whose - and I walk between the tall trees that cast a shadow over the road and me. The thick and dark forest is waiting for my prayer.

"Holy Mary," I kneel and whisper again, feeling the cold ground that dampens my knees. "I'm giving up on him. No matter where he is, alive or in your gentle arms, please watch over him," I whisper, and can't hold back my tears. "I have a son to raise, and I've failed. Please, watch over him. I'm going back home."

I gently dig in the moist soil with my fingers, place the German gun inside. I don't want its protection anymore. Then, I kiss the statue of the Virgin and put it on the grass, rise to my feet, and notice the few rays of sunlight that break through the treetops and hear birds chirping. Maybe it's a sign, but I don't know anymore. I know that I need to get on my motorcycle and ride back home now, without looking back. I have a child waiting for me, and I've failed.

Tea with Grandma
November 2021, Kyiv, Ukraine

Anna

"Grandma, come sit down, have some tea." I hand her the hot mug and sit down at her side. I help her with the sugar cube and watch as her wrinkled fingers gently stir the spoon in the hot teacup. It started snowing again, and mom asked me to come over and see how she was doing. Maybe I shouldn't talk to her about that picture of the woman anymore. Perhaps we should leave the past behind.

"You know, Anuchka," she looks at me after a while. Her eyes are bloodshot. "He was very weak and sick. At first, I hated him when he was brought in with three other prisoners to help us on the farm in the fall of 1945."

The Prisoner of War
September 1945, a farm east of Kyiv, five months after the war ended

Maria (Mariusha)

The Red Army's military truck slowly drives in and pulls over at the center of our farm's front yard, causing the chickens to scatter in a storm of feathers and hide in the wild weeds surrounding the barn and the muddy pigsty. Father and I come out of our hut and notice a young officer stepping out of the truck and walking towards us. He's about my age, in his early twenties, and has a well-kept black mustache. I look at his officer's visor hat and his proud walk, as if he had just completed his education at the commanders' academy.

"Yafimovna family?" The officer asks as he approaches us.

"Yes," father and I reply, examining his clean uniform. The driver also comes out of the vehicle, and lights himself a cigarette. He leans against the parked truck and fills the air with the foul smell of cheap tobacco. I look at the truck covered in mud, as if it had traveled a long way, and the rear of the vehicle is covered with an old green tarp with the red star prominently painted on it. What does the officer want from us?

"In the name of the regional committee and the communist people, we're placing in your care four prisoners of war. They'll work in your farm." He pulls out a folded paper and hands it to father. "Please sign here that you've received them."

"And what should we do with them?" father inquires.

"Work them to death." The officer laughs. "No one's taking them back, but from now on, you must meet your crop quotas. The war is over."

"Mariusha, sign it," Father says to me. He hands me the papers and pen, and I sign the document as I examine the papers' title and sickle-and-hammer seals that have been stamped on in red ink. 'Prisoners of war aid the Soviet people.'

"Get out." The officer knocks on the rear of the truck. A hand stretches out from under the tarpaulin cover, moving it aside, and four people slowly come out; one by one, their feet touch the ground, trying to remain steady. Finally, they line up and look at us.

They're thin, and their glare is hollow and indifferent as they stand and look around in silence. I approach and examine them, the human monsters who attacked us in the war. For a moment, I try to stop myself, but then I don't hold back and walk past them again, spitting at their face one after the other.

Three of them are fair-haired and taller than me. They're dressed in worn out gray-green uniforms, and their shoulders are covered in remnants of rank insignia, which have been torn off long ago. The fourth one is a slightly different from the rest. He has black hair and dark eyes and is also taller than me. He's unshaven and dressed in a different khaki uniform than the others; it's also tattered. I stop in front of him and look at his thin body as he examines me, ignoring the saliva on his cheek.

"What do we do if they try to escape?" I ask the Red Army officer.

"They won't," he says as he heads to the truck. "They're too weak. They don't stand a chance reaching the border and certainly not Germany. If any of them escape, the NKVD will easily catch them and take them to a firing squad."

"Excellent." I approach him and return the signed papers, waiting patiently while he carefully examines my signature.

"Nice to meet you, comrade Maria," he shakes my hand. "I'm in charge of the area on behalf of the army and the party."

"Nice to meet you too," I shake his hand warmly and examine his ironed uniform with the symbol of the Communist Party attached to his chest.

"If there's a problem, just let me know, and I'll take care of the rest." He climbs into the truck and slams the door shut. The driver throws the cigarette on the ground and climbs in after him. "Don't forget; from now on, you have to meet the new crop quotas," he says as the truck starts with a screeching rumble, and the chickens in the yard once again scatter everywhere.

"Mariusha, they're under your responsibility," father says to me and walks away after the truck leaves the yard. He's heading to the barn to fix the wagon frame that broke yesterday. I look at them standing in front of me, motionless as if uncaring as to what we do to them.

"Where will we house them?" I yell at him.

"In the pigsty," he yells back. "That's where they should be after what they did to us in the war."

"Get up. Time to work," I wake them up every day at dusk when I go to feed the pigs. The pigs get their food, as do the men; I throw at each of them a loaf of bread. In the evening, I give them grits soup. They sleep in the corner of the pigsty on old burlap sacks filled with hay. The three prisoners with the green-gray uniforms sleep on one side of the sty, and the black-haired one a little further from them. Why does he sleep alone?

After I feed the pigs, I harness the old horse to the wooden wagon. Father had hidden it in the woods during the war and the German occupation. I wait for the prisoners to come out and climb into the back, and we head to the fields to plow the land before winter.

"Start moving," I shout at them as they harness themselves to the simple plow and begin to pull it across the field, replacing the two horses that were taken in the war when the enemy arrived and plundered every animal they could find.

They slowly drag the plow on the moist soil, panting and advancing step by step, while the plow's blade carves a deep furrow. I follow them, holding the reins and scattering the wheat kernels in the ground.

"Away!" I stop every now and then and throw stones at the birds that gather behind me and nibble the seeds I had scattered on the moist ground. "Fly away!" I momentarily let go of the reins, and run after them, watching them flap with their wings and disappear in the distance. We have to meet next summer's wheat quotas.

"Keep walking!" I grab the reins again and prompt the prisoners. "We used to have two horses that your German army took from us," I scold them from time to time, but I don't think they care at all. They don't answer or even turn their heads. They just continue to pull the plow indifferently, slowly walking step by step through the plowed field while I watch their hunched and sweaty backs. Maybe in a few months we'll receive a new tractor from the big factory in Stalingrad, where I had once worked before the Germans destroyed it.

"Take it," I hand them the steel water jug when we stop to rest, throwing the enamel cups at them. Despite the cool autumn breeze, their uniforms are stained with sweat. They sip from the water and eat the bread they had received in the morning as they quietly speak in German to one another.

"Go away," I yell at the birds again, and chase them across the field, throwing stones at them. "Fly away," I wave my arms before I turn back and try to catch my breath. I start walking towards the horse and wagon patiently awaiting me at the edge of the field next to the prisoners on their break.

We work together, day after day, and I urge them so that we can finish plowing before winter comes. If we don't finish in time, the ground will freeze, and we won't be able to plow anymore. But one day, when I walk in the field back to the wagon after having chased away a flock of birds, I hear music playing.

It's neither a happy nor a sad tune, and even though I've never heard it, I find it pleasant. I walk slowly towards the music, passing through the dirt, and looking for the man playing the music.

He's sitting with his back to me, away from the other three Germans. When I approach, I see a harmonica between his lips. I draw closer; his eyes are shut, and his fingers gently flutter on the metal box. He stops and coughs, but a few seconds later, he shuts his eyes again and resumes playing. Even the others stop talking and listen. I want to shut my eyes too and listen to the music, forget the other POWs, the old horse and the work that still has to be completed before winter comes.

"Stop," I say to him, and he opens his eyes and looks at me. After a moment, he wipes his harmonica with his sleeve and stuffs it back into his shirt pocket without saying a word. "We have more work to do." I move away from them towards the plow parked on the side of the field, hearing him cough again.

In the following days, I make sure to chase the birds in the field when we stop to rest. I try to walk as far away from them as I can, hoping that when I get back, I'll hear him play again.

"Where's the other one?" I ask the three Germans when I bring their bread on Sunday morning. It'll rain later today, and we won't be going out to the field. They're at their corner in the pigsty, but he isn't there. The burlap sacks he'd sleep on are still there.

"He left," one of them says in Russian.

"What do you mean 'left'?" I approach them. Did he run away?

"He left. He was gone when we woke up," he replies. "Maybe he's in the fields."

"Yes, perhaps," I kick the empty burlap sacks in his corner, but I find nothing there but a huff of dust and a small pencil. I grab the pencil and put it in my pocket, rushing out of the pigsty. He ran away. I have to report him to the officer in charge on behalf of the party.

"Let's take care of the missing German," I whisper to the old horse, and offer it a sugar cube straight out of my palm, feeling it gently lick the sugar off my hand. Then I place the saddle on the steed, fasten the leather strap, and reward it with another sugar cube. "Let's go," I mount the horse and ride out of the farm and into the village, thinking about what I'd say to the officer. No one likes German fugitives.

The horse is too old to gallop, and I don't prompt it to as it trots down the muddy path. I watch the clouds gathering in the sky. Perhaps he hasn't ran away and he simply went out to the fields and will soon come back? Perhaps I'm rushing to report him? My gaze scans the area, searching for him.

"Stop, let's stay here for a few minutes," I instruct the horse and carefully direct it to the plowed field, through the muddy ground so it doesn't trip. "Let's look for the German harmonica player," I say to the horse. Every now and then, I stop and try to listen, but I can only hear the birds chirping, and the leaves on the trees at the edge of the field rustle gently.

"Let's head to the village. The German prisoner ran away." I pet my faithful horse and turn it to the path leading to the village. But then I see him in the distance, crouching between the bushes.

He hides quietly, almost motionless, close to the ground. I dismount my horse, tie the reins to one of the trees at the edge of the field, and approach him on foot.

"What are you doing?" I finally ask him, noticing the fluttering bird in his hands. It's still alive

He stares at me and doesn't reply. The bird is still in his hands. I notice bird traps in the bushes. He must have hunted it.

"These birds belong to the Soviet people. You have no right to hunt them."

"These birds don't belong to anyone," he replies as he gently caresses the bird's wing. "Birds are free."

"How do you speak Russian?" I approach him.

"I spent three years in a POW camp. I learned Russian," he looks at me, still crouching.

"Stand up," I say, and he slowly stands up, bird still in hand. He's thin and unshaven, and his old uniform is muddy.

"What's that?" I notice something attached to the bird's leg. I take a few steps closer to him with my hand outstretched. "Why are you hunting them?"

"I set them free," he answers with a wave of his hand as I approach. The bird spreads its wings and flies away, and I follow it with my gaze as it disappears behind the trees. "What did you do to the bird? What did you connect to it? Clear out your pockets," I stand close to him and look straight into his dark eyes, smelling his body odor and unclean uniform.

"Here you go." He puts his hand in his pocket and pulls out some used rifle brass shells and an iron wire.

"What is it?" I take the used cases from his hand, examine them and using my fingernails, I remove the piece of rolled-up paper tucked into one of them. I unfold it. There are several sentences on it in a foreign language. "What are you doing with these notes? Are you a spy?"

"I'm not a spy." He stares at me.

"I'll report you. You're a prisoner, a murderer, and a spy. You deserve to die."

"I'm not a murderer," he says and coughs. "I've shot trees, I've shot the ground, I've shot the sky, but I've never shot anyone," he speaks slowly, as if trying to pick the right words in Russian. "Maybe I deserve to die because I marched into your country, but I won't die because I shot someone."

"Why aren't you with them? With the others?" I hold onto the empty cases, examining the shiny copper. What is he hiding?

"Because they don't like strangers."

"Aren't you German?"

"It doesn't matter. In your eyes, I'm German," he answers and coughs again.

"Where are you from?"

"Does it matter?"

"No, it doesn't matter to me. You're an enemy of the communist people. That's enough." I turn and walk away from him and towards the horse. "I'll report you. The officer will be happy to know what I've found."

When I untie my horse and mount it preparing to ride to the village, I look back for a moment at the German prisoner, expecting him to flee. However, he stays put, motionless, staring at me, his hands at his sides. The officer will know what to do with him.

There are a couple of carts and some burnt houses in the village center, a reminder of the German occupation. But the red hammer and sickle flag waves proudly over the committee building. I steer the horse in that direction, but then stop. What does it say on the note he hid in the brass cartridge?

"The note is in Italian," the village doctor tells me. His wrinkled fingers uncrumple the note, then he puts on his glasses, leans in, and examines it.

"What does it say?"

"It's a note to a woman who lives in a village south of Rome. The note says that if anyone finds this message tied to the bird's leg, they should tell his wife that he's alive."

"And it doesn't say that he's trying to escape?" I watch the doctor bringing the note closer to his eyes.

"No, just to tell her that he's alive and loves her." He takes his glasses off and looks at me.

"What's the woman's name?"

"Does it matter?" He hands me the paper back. "Who wrote the note?"

"It doesn't matter. I found it tied to a dead bird's leg. Thank you, doctor." I fold the note, leave the clinic, and return to my horse.

He isn't where I've left him in the field, and the traps hidden in the bushes are also empty. But when I arrive at the farm and tie up the horse, I walk past the pigsty and hear a harmonica playing.

"Play for me," I say to him later that evening when I bring them their pot of semolina soup and place it in the corner. The other three German prisoners approach me and take their portion, return to their corner, and watch us in silence.

"You can't order someone to play for you," he stays in his place and doesn't get up to take his soup.

"Play for me, please." I pour some of the soup into the enamel bowl and hand it to him, but he doesn't lift his arm, and I place the bowl on the cold ground next to him.

He brings the harmonica to his lips and plays a melody, which is neither happy nor sad; I like it. Under the lantern's dim light, I watch his fingers hold the harmonica between his lips while he leans against the wooden wall at the corner of the pigsty. Who is the woman he loves?

When he finishes playing and turns to eat his soup, I leave his note and the brass cartridge on the floor, as well as four pieces of coarse hand soap I brought from home and a stainless-steel bucket for water. I also tell them to move their things to the old barn on the other side of the yard.

On Sundays, when it doesn't snow, I look for him in the fields, and ask him to play for me, but other than that, we don't talk. He's the enemy, and he has a woman that he loves.

"I can see they're still alive," the young officer inspects them a few months later. An early morning summer sun shines down on the four prisoners sitting on the wood wagon drawn by the old horse. They're ready to go out to the fields.

"Yes, they're still alive." I look at him and at his clean ironed clothes. He entered the farm driving a military jeep just as we were about to head out to the fields. He's standing very close to me. A decoration of 'The Order of the Patriotic War' is pinned to his chest, glistening in the sun.

"And what about you, comrade Maria?" He smiles at me as I look at his neat mustache.

"What about me?"

"What about a husband? Don't you think it's time you found a proper husband? Being single isn't good."

"We don't have many men left after the war. You know

that. That's our fate, us women." I reach out and grab the papers he hands me. I look at them, examining the harvest quotas for this coming summer.

"Yes, too many men didn't return from the battlefields," he agrees. "But I came back. I fought the Nazi monsters, and I came back."

"You increased the quotas this year." I show him the paper. "We harvested less last year."

"Yes, the Soviet economy needs to recover, and you have them," he gestures at the wagon. "You didn't just get them. They're supposed to sacrifice their lives for the prosperity of the Soviet Union. Set a daily quota for them. They're Germans; they like orders." He scrutinizes them, as the prisoners on the wagon stare indifferently, as if the conversation doesn't concern them.

"We'll manage." I retrieve the papers.

"The party knows you'll figure it out." He folds the papers and stuffs them into his pocket. "Comrade Maria, the party's committee occasionally organizes a dance in the village. I'd be happy for you to come." He shakes my hand and walks to his clean military jeep.

"I'll come," I reply.

"Comrade Maria, I'd love to dance with you." He waves goodbye and gets into the jeep. I follow him as he starts the engine and drives away until he disappears behind the barn and the pigsty. He isn't a bad man.

I silently climb into the wagon and lead the horse to the wheat field, as I examine the ripe golden ears of wheat gently swaying in the breeze.

"Wait here," I say to the prisoners jumping off the wagon as I walk to the edge of the field. I collect a few branches and stick them in the ground at a distance from each other. "This is the area each of you must reap every day," I instruct them as we take the scythes and begin to work under the sun. The German army also took our agricultural machines during the war, but the Red Army officer promised that in a year or two, we'll receive new ones.

I bend over and hold my scythe tightly, harvesting the wheat in circular motions, and gathering the scattered wheat into bundles, as sweat trickles down my face. The others work in silence, each in his own section. All I can hear is him coughing from time to time; his coughs echo over the sounds of the crickets and cicadas. By the end of the day, when I finish my section, I lift my head and look around. The other three rest by the wagon under the shade; the wheat they harvested is stacked in neat bundles. He's the only one still working, his hands wield the scythe again and again, but occasionally, he stops and coughs before he continues.

"Father, the party has given us new quotas," I tell him while we have dinner in the kitchenette.

"That's how they do things in Moscow. They rob us of all the wheat before they let us live," he dips the rye bread into the bowl of potato stew.

"I divided the field. Each prisoner has his own quota."

"That's good." He takes a bite from the bread. "We're lucky we got them."

"One of them is weaker than the others," I smear butter on a big slice of bread.

"Report him. Talk to the officer in charge; the one with the nice uniform." He takes another slice. "He surely knows how to deal with the German vermin."

"Yes, surely he'll know what to do with him." I slowly chew the slice of bread and examine my callused hand after a long day of hard fieldwork.

At night, before I get into bed, I prepare the prisoners' bread for tomorrow. I knead the dough, divide it into four quarters and let it rise. Father's asleep and has turned off the main room lantern. I open the small cupboard and grab several sugar cubes, the same ones we feed the horse daily. I crumble the sugar and mix it into one dough quarters, finally carving a large cross on it, to set it apart from the others.

"Wake up. It's time to work," I wake them up the following day and give them their bread, making sure that he receives the one I had carved. At the end of the day, at dusk, he has yet again failed to meet his quota. I place my bundle of wheat by the cart and go over to help him. It's not a lot of work for me.

We work side by side in silence. The peace is disturbed only by our heavy breaths, and the swishes of the scythe we monotonously swing to harvest the wheat. I raise my head occasionally and look at him, examining his sweaty face and his heavy breathing. His cough isn't getting any better. I'll try adding more sugar into the bread I'll bake tonight.

"Thank you," he says at the end of the day, as we reach the stick in the ground marking his daily quota area. But I don't answer him and walk away through the field, starting to bundle the wheat. No one can know that I'm helping a prisoner of war.

But even in the following days, despite the sugar in the bread and my help at the end of each day, he's getting ever weaker, and I have to work by his side even more and make sure to keep my distance from him of fear that someone will pass by the dirt path leading to the farm and see us working close to one another.

"Wake up. It's time for work," I wake them up a few days later, place his bread in the corner, and make sure he receives his allotted loaf. I then go out and wait for them outside, by the wagon, as the horse quietly neighs, watching the rays of sun begin to burst on the horizon.

"Where is he?" I ask the three Germans who come out of the barn. "Why doesn't he come out?" But they don't reply and silently climb into the cart, rubbing their hands together to keep warm.

"Wait for me here," I say to them and go back into the barn. What happened to him?

He keeps lying on the burlap sacks and watches me as I get close and stand over him.

"You must go to work," I say to him.

"I'm sorry," he coughs and weakly replies, still looking at me.

"You have to get up," I bend down and touch his leg with mine. "Otherwise, I'll have to report you," I touch him again. "Please, get up," but he just keeps looking at me and coughs again. It's not my problem. He's a replaceable prisoner of war brought here to work himself to death. I look at him for one more minute, examine his sweaty face. His chest rises and falls with every breath he takes while he lies on the burlap bags in his worn-out uniform. I turn and leave the barn towards the cart. I have work to do. The Soviet economy has to meet its quotas.

"Start working. I'll be right back," I say to the three Germans after arriving at the field, marking the daily quota they have to harvest for them. "Let's go," I urge the horse, even though it's walking slowly on the dirt road leading to the village. I must handle the prisoner of war who didn't get up for work. I stop the cart near the committee building, watching the red flag hanging in front of it, and rush to the doctor's house on the other side of the road. Maybe he'll agree to come and see the prisoner before I have to report it to the Red Army officer.

"Where is he?" he asks me, holding his medical bag as we arrive to the farm, and he gets out of the wagon.

"Come with me. He's here," I walk towards the barn.

"Where are you going?" He stops and looks at me.

"I have someone here who needs help. He's sick and won't stop coughing."

"Who are they? The filthy mice? The ones who destroyed our nation?"

"Please, doctor," I try to think what to say to him.

"Is that why you brought me all the way out here?" He turns and climbs back into the wagon, placing his large, brown, leather medical bag beside him on the bench.

"He's a workhorse," I say to him. "I need him alive to harvest the wheat. Mother Russia needs to use him to work the field," I stand next to the cart and look up at him. He must help him.

"Have you forgotten what they did to us?"

"I didn't forget. I was there too. I was in Stalingrad. I know exactly who they are," I reply. I mustn't think about the gray-green uniformed Germans from that winter. I should only think about that sick man in my barn. He won't survive if the doctor doesn't treat him. "And he's not German," I add.

"I don't care if he's German or not. He's one of them," he says. "Is that the man who wrote the note?"

"No," I hasten to answer. "The note I showed you is from a dead Italian soldier I found at Stalingrad when I was there, from a filthy rat," I spit on the ground. He mustn't suspect anything, so he won't report me.

"And who's this?" He's watching me. What should I tell him?

"I think he's an Austrian," I quickly say and spit again.

"They're the same as the Germans. I'm not wasting our country's precious medicine on him. I'll never check him," he angrily says. "Please take me back to the village. I have patients waiting for me."

"Could you please check the horse? It sometimes limps. I think it has an infection," I hold the old horse's reins and gently stroke his nose.

"I'm a people doctor, not a veterinarian."

"I know it's the kind of things you do," I watch him.

"That's not my job. My job is only to treat people. I'm a doctor of the soviet people."

"Wait a minute," I turn around and walk to the pigsty. There's something I have to do. "Can you accept this gift from the Communist people?" I return after a few minutes, panting and tightly holding a small pig in my arms. I place it in the cart, tying to prevent it from running away. We'll manage without him. The doctor sighs, gets off the wagon, and starts examining the horse. I remain sitting in the wagon, next to the doctor's leather bag, watching as he bends down to examine the horse's legs and takes out two glass vials with the word "penicillin" written on them.

"Your horse is old, but it seems fine to me," he says after a few minutes. "Don't call me to take care of these filthy rats again," he climbs into the cart and sits next to me.

"Thank you, doctor, for agreeing to come," I hold the reins and spur the horse, hoping he won't check his medical bag.

Come nighttime, after Father falls asleep, I take the lantern and go to the barn. I walk to his corner, using the lantern's weak light to find my way. I place it on the floor so its light won't wake the Germans up.

"You must get better," I sit down next to him.

He doesn't answer me but opens his eyes, breathes and weakly coughs.

"Drink," I pour water into an enamel cup and serve it to him, but he brings the cup to his lips and doesn't take a sip. "You must drink," I reach out and touch him for the first time, holding the back of his neck as I help him sit up.

"Thank you," he whispers and sips a bit of water.

"Drink it," I hand him a vial of penicillin, and he sips the clear liquid. I don't have a syringe, and even if I had, I wouldn't know how to inject it. I can only let him drink the medicine, hoping it'll help him.

"Thank you," he whispers to me again and hands me the empty vial.

"You need to get better," I tell him. "You won't last until the end of the summer," I try to bring a bowl of soup closer to his mouth.

"I know," he places the bowl on the hard ground without

taking a sip. "You should report me for no longer being effective."

"Just drink the soup," I take a spoon and try to bring it closer to his mouth, but he lies back and turns his back to me. In the dim lantern light, I notice his hand searching in the burlap sacks on which he lies.

"Take it, please," he hands me something, and I can feel the hard paper and notice it's a picture.

"Who is she?" I look at the woman in the photo, she's standing next to a motorcycle.

"Please, send it to her"

"What should I send?" I turn the photo over, something is written on the back, but I can't read it in the faint light.

"A letter on my behalf. Tell her that I love her."

"I can't send her a letter," I whisper. "You can't send letters outside the Soviet Union. The censorship won't approve them." I try to hand him back the picture, but he pushes my hand away.

"Please." He fumbles through the burlap sack again and pulls out a couple of small pieces of papers and a used rifle brass cartridge. He places the papers in my palm and closes my fist. "Please," he whispers again and coughs.

I wipe his sweaty forehead with a damp cloth, get up and leave the barn, holding the lantern in one hand and feeling the cold brass cartridge in my warm fist.

What should I do?

The sun starts to rise in the east as I kneel among the bushes, place pieces of bread in the traps, and take a step back, searching for the birds chirping around. I have to return to the farm, wake them up, and go to work. In the soft morning light, my gaze follows a bird approaching the slice, moving toward it in leaps.

"Please," I whisper to it. "Please."

Another jump and another step, it approaches to peck at the bread and gets caught. I draw closer, put my hands on its wings that flutter in fear, and gather it into my lap.

"Don't be afraid," I tell the bird as I caress it gently. I examine its black eyes, staring at me with fear. "I'll send you on your way soon."

I wrap the iron wire around its leg and attach the brass cartridge. I tuck inside one of the rolled-up notes he had given me. Earlier, at home, I sealed the opening of the cartridge with wax so that the note wouldn't fall out.

"Go fly, find her." I release the bird, and it spreads its wings and takes off. However, a couple of seconds later, the bird falls to the ground. "Fly, get out of here." I approach the bird and pick it up again, throwing it into the air. But it flaps its wings and once again falls on the moist ground. The brass cartridge is too heavy for the small creature. "You should be free. Fly wherever you want." I remove the iron wire from its leg and watch the bird take off and disappear beyond the trees at the edge of the field. I shove the cartridge into my pocket and walk back to the horse. I tried as best as I could. Now I have to return to the farm and wake them up for work. We have harvest quotas to meet.

Before I mount the horse, I look back at the fields that haven't been harvested yet. I can't leave him in the barn and give him time to recover. I must report him.

"Get up." I whisper to him in the middle of the night and nudge his shoulder, then shine the lantern's dim light on his face. The other three Germans are asleep in their corner.

"Did you send it?" He opens his eyes and looks at me.

"You need to get up." I lean over and help him up. We must hurry. Earlier that day, I had to go to the village and meet with the officer.

"What are you doing?"

"Come with me." I pull him to his feet, ignoring the smell of his dirty uniform as I support him and touch his tattered clothes. The penicillin helped him a little, but he's still too weak. I leave the barn and climb into the wagon, petting my loyal horse. He follows me and then stops, staring at me in the dark.

"Where are you taking me to?"

"To a new place," I reply. He mustn't know where we're going. The NKVD patrols are watching the roads and examining certificates and transit permissions.

"Did you report me? Is this the end?" He stays put.

"Please, hop on," I say to him, wiping a tear away. Thankfully, it's too dark for him to notice my crying.

He struggles to climb into the wagon, so I get down to help him and ask him to lean on my shoulder while he climbs up.

"I'll manage on my own. I marched proudly into this war, and I'll march proudly out of it," he replies, refusing to take my hand and holding onto the wagon, supporting himself up as he coughs.

"Take this, drink up," I hand him the second penicillin vial as he sits down on the burlap sacks that are full of hay and which I had prepared for him in the back of the wagon. "Lie down," I whisper to him, holding the reins and clicking my tongue to urge the horse to start walking. We have a long way to go.

"Halt," I order the horse a few days later on the side of the road and observe the wooden barn and the barrier in the distance.

I can see the soldier at the guard post next to the checkpoint. Then I notice the red flag of the hammer and sickle gently waving in the morning breeze. There are barbed wire fences all around, and I think I can notice a military jeep parked next to the barrier. We've reached the end of the journey.

"Take these, put them on." I turn to the back of the wagon. Then, I reach into one of the sacks and fish out clothes I had stolen from my father. "I hope they fit you." I also hope that father will understand and forgive me. I left a note for him on the kitchen table explaining what I had done.

"What is this place?" He asks me as he begins to strip off his old uniform. His cough has improved a little in the last few days. Perhaps resting in the wagon had helped him.

"From here, you continue on your own," I say and turn my gaze, looking at the border station again. I don't want to embarrass him as he removes his torn uniform. I notice another soldier in the distance. He's approaching the guard position and talking to the soldier inside. It seems to me that they're laughing, though I can't tell what they're saying.

"Take this," I pull an old leather backpack out of the sack. "I packed a few army biscuits and some provisions for the road, at least for some of it."

"Do I look okay?" He asks me, and I turn to look at him. He's dressed in simple work clothes and looks like a poor peasant. He's so thin.

"Hang on, put this on," I go through the sacks and find a piece of rope. He ties it as a belt so that his blue pants don't fall off.

"Thank you," he says and hops off the cart, stands on the path, and hangs the leather backpack on his shoulder.

"Wait, this is for you." I open the two top buttons of my simple laborer's shirt and pull an identification card out of my bra. I hand it to him.

"What is it?" He takes the card, and I momentarily feel the touch of his fingers. "What does it say?" He opens it and looks at the letters and seals.

"It says that you're a Jewish refugee who fled to the Soviet Union during the war, and now you're returning to your homeland, Italy."

"Is it real? Will they let me pass through?"

"Yes," I reply and glance at the soldiers at the guard post. "This is a real document."

"How did you get it?"

"It doesn't matter," I say. "Start walking so they won't notice us and become suspicious."

"Thank you for everything," he says for the last time and begins to walk slowly on the road leading to the border station.

I remain sitting on the cart and watch him from a distance as he approaches the guard post, stops, and starts talking to one of the soldiers. One of them moves away and returns a moment later with another soldier. I think he's an officer. I need to turn around and get away, so they don't notice me and start asking him more questions.

"Go home," I click my tongue at the horse and let go of the reins, and it slowly takes a turn. We have a long way home. I rub my bloodshot eyes; they sting because of the morning wind. For a moment, I'm tempted to look back and see if he made it through, but the trees conceal the station and I notice his old uniform. He left it carefully folded and on the haystack at the back of the wagon, he had also left his harmonica on top of the pile.

Later, when the border station is in the distance, I see a small nook hidden among the trees, with a statue of Mary in a small wooden booth. I stop the wagon and get off the path, approach and kneel.

"Holy Mary," I cross myself and close my eyes, "please, make sure that he survives the long way home and returns to the woman he loves, and please, make sure the Communist Committee officer will be a good husband. I know he's a good man. He listened to me and agreed to help me. Therefore, I'll accept his proposal." I open my eyes and notice the rays of sun seeping through the trees. "And please, I hope that someday I'll sit with my grandchildren and tell them my story and be proud of what I did. I'm not sure I've done the right thing. Tell me, did I do the right thing?" I close my eyes again, but Holy Mary doesn't reply, and all I can hear are the birds chirping around.

Summer
Summer of 1946, Italy, a year after the war ended

Francesca

'**At the American martial law order, starting in the summer of 1946, a democratic constituent assembly would be established for the Italian nation, and the military government would end.**'

I watch the worker, dressed in blue, hanging the poster on the bulletin board. He's holding a brush and applying a thick coat of glue from the bucket in his other hand.

Two or three more brush strokes of glue over the paper and he's on his way down the street. I stay behind to look at the new poster, droplets of the wet glue still glistening in the morning's sun.

The street is quiet during these early hours, and I glance across the alley to see that no one's coming before I approach the bulletin board and pretend to read it.

"Mom, what are you doing?" Raffaele asks me.

"I'm playing," I tell him as I rip off the poster, tearing the paper into small pieces. "Don't you want to try it too?"

"It sticks to my hand," he laughs as he rolls the pieces of paper between his little hands.

"It's funny, isn't it?" I laugh with him and roll the papers into balls. "Throw the paper balls as far as you can," I give him another piece of paper. "It's fun," I help him throw away the rolled-up paper, watch it hitting the cobblestones, and look up.

And then I see him.

He walks slowly, approaching us, step-by-step on the pavement, not taking his eyes off me the entire time. The neat military uniform I'd stroked the last time I saw him has been replaced by a tattered peasant cloth tied with a simple rope, and his black hair, which was once combed and oiled in a fashionable way, is wild and untidy.

Is that him? Is that my man?

I reach out my hand and support myself, leaning on the bulletin board and the torn poster, placing my other hand on Raffaele's head.

"Mom, why are you crying?" Raffaele raises his eyes to me and asks.

"I've returned," he stands in front of me, and I look at his dark eyes and the redness in them.

"I've been looking for you," I caress his thin face, my fingers gently stroking his stubble.

"I tried to send you letters," he places his hand on my trembling fingers.

"I couldn't find you," my finger touches a tear rolling down his cheek.

"I didn't believe I'd be back," he puts both hands on my waist, and I'm momentarily ashamed of being so thin. There's still very little food in the village.

"Mom, who's this man?" I hear Raffaele as he holds on to my leg.

"You have a child," I wrap my arms around him, press against his body, and gently kiss his neck.

"I have a child?" I feel his body shaking.

"We have a child," my lips touch his.

He stops hugging me and leans towards Raffaele, slowly stroking his hair.

"Mom?" I feel Raffaele grab the hem of my dress.

"This is your father. This is my man." I start kissing him gently.

The End

Author's Notes, Pieces of History

The Fascist rule in Italy began in 1922, when Benito Mussolini, called 'The Duce,' came to power.

His men, the Black Shirts, terrorized the Italians who tried to oppose them. Francesca's father, who tried to protest and resist, was beaten and probably murdered by them although they claim he died in a car accident.

Throughout his rule, from 1922 to 1943, the Duce sent the Italian army to many conflicts, believing Italy would become an empire again. But the Italian soldiers weren't very motivated and fought poorly. When WWII broke out, Hitler invaded Belgium and France. Mussolini joined him, declaring war against the Allies, believing he'd rule the world alongside Hitler. The war declaration is the first poster that Francesca tears at the beginning of the book. The Italian soldiers were sent to North Africa to fight against the British, where Cecilia's husband was killed, in the battle of El-Alamein, Egypt. And finally, an Italian army corps joined the German army in 1941 as they invaded Russia.

"Operation Barbarossa" was the code name for the German attack against the Russians in the summer of 1941, the goal of which was the conquest of the Communist Soviet Union. The newspaper boy mentions this attack the day Emanuele boards the train. However, the operation failed and in December 1941, after reaching the outskirts of Moscow, the Germans were forced to retreat due to Russian counterattacks and the harsh winter. Emanuele didn't participate in the battles and was instead stationed in Yugoslavia on guard missions, where the Italian army assisted the German army.

In the summer of 1942, the Germans launched another attack against Russia called "Operation Blue," to conquer southern Russia, including the city of Stalingrad. This attack is mentioned in the newspaper that's on the floor on the day Francesca gives birth to Raffaele. A large Italian expeditionary force was added to this attack to assist the Germans. Among them was Emanuele. Still, after heavy fighting, in November 1942, the Russians surrounded about a quarter of a million German and Italian soldiers in Stalingrad. With the coming of winter, many of them froze to death.

The Germans refused to admit that their forces were besieged and destroyed in the Russian snow. This can be seen by the Italian Ministry of Defense clerk's reaction during Francesca's first visit to Rome. He scolds her for spreading false rumors.

Finally, in February 1943, about one hundred thousand surviving soldiers surrendered to the Russian army and were captured; most of them died in POW camps due to their poor physical condition.

When the American army invaded southern Italy, in 1943, Mussolini was deposed, and the Italians signed an armistice with the Americans. However, the Germans rushed to take control of most of Italy's territory and set up defensive lines in the mountains. This is seen in the book when their presence in the village increases, and they establish a military airbase nearby, using forced laborers brought from the countries they'd conquered.

In the winter of 1943, the Americans advanced from Naples toward Rome. It is in this attack that the village was liberated and Gabriele is killed. Later, Francesca starts working at the army hospital and meets Grace, an American nurse who was injured; she is the heroine of the book The Wounded Nurse. In this book, I wrote a slightly different plot for Grace and Francesca, to illuminate their relationship from Francesca's point of view.

The breach of the German lines and occupation of Rome took place in August 1944, a few days later, Francesca and Grace go on Francesca's second journey to Rome. This time they visit Emanuele's family and try once again to get information at the Ministry of Defense before an American officer tries to help her.

The Germans manage to hold defensive lines in northern Italy right up to the end of the war. Francesca's journey to Russia could only take place a few months after the war ends, with the stabilization of the borders and the start of the refugees movement on the roads.

The Communist Soviet Union treated prisoners of war terribly, in response to the horrible German attack that caused millions of losses. Those who survive are worked to death after the war. Many of them are sent to labor camps in Siberia or to Stalingrad to rebuild the destroyed city. I chose to send Emanuele and three other German prisoners of war to a farm in Ukraine, where Maria (Mariusha) meets him and finally brings him to the border and save his life.

During Francesca's journey to Russia, before the border station, she meets a group of refugees. These refugees are Jewish concentration camp Holocaust survivors. After the war ends, many of them - having lost their families and loved ones - begin to migrate in groups toward Italy and southern France. There they board dilapidated ships and sail as illegal immigrants to the State of Israel, at the time still under British rule and called Palestine.

During the WWII, the Communist government ruled the entire Soviet Union, included Ukraine, under Stalin. Only in 1991, with the dissolution of the Soviet Union, did Ukraine gain independence. 2014 Vladimir Putin, the president of Russia, began making territorial demands of Ukraine. On February 24th, 2022, six months after Anuchka finds the photo of the woman on the motorcycle, Russian forces invade Ukraine with the intention of conquering it and annexing it to Russian rule once again.

At the time of writing this book, Ukrainian forces are still fighting bravely, succeeding in stopping and repelling the Russian army. To this day, I don't understand why dictators haven't learned from history - that attempts to conquer other countries only bring death and destruction.

In this book, I chose to give the men names with religious meaning. All names originated from the Hebrew language and were transferred into Italian.

Emanuele – the meaning of the name in Hebrew is 'God with us,' or 'God with him.'

Gabriele – the meaning of the name in Hebrew is 'Man of God.' Gabriele is mentioned in the Bible as an angel and a God's messenger. In the book, the villagers think that Gabriele was a madman, but he wasn't crazy at all. Gabriele is a former WWI soldier who'd suffered from post-traumatic stress as a result of the war twenty-five years earlier. Even though everyone thinks he's crazy, he's the one that tries to warn them of the coming disaster.

Raffaele – the meaning of the name in Hebrew is 'God will heal you.'

Throughout the book, I avoided describing the horrors of this terrible war and tried to show that there were good people on both warring sides, whether it's Emanuele, Francesca, Grace, the American officer at the Italian Ministry of Defense, Maria, or Nikolai, the Russian officer at the border station. I believe that good is inside all of us and that we must choose between good and evil in times of war.

I couldn't be precise in all the historical details I wrote in the book, but for me, writing it was a fascinating journey in the story of a woman who fought to bring her husband back from the bleeding battlefields of WWII.

Thank you for reading.

Alex Amit

Printed in Great Britain
by Amazon